Who Needs an Oil Well?

Who Needs an Oil Well?

Ruth Unrau

Drawings by Jan Gleysteen

ABINGDON PRESS

Nashville New York

Printed in the United States of America
Library of Congress Catalog Card No. 68-15405

For Walt
and his dozens
of cousins

Dear Reader:

This is not a true story and the people in it are made up. The one exception is Donald, if you want to call him people. He was real.

There are some true situations in the story, however. Oklahoma in the 1930's had many bank robberies, some of them pulled by Charles "Pretty Boy" Floyd. His home was in northeastern Oklahoma and he spent part of his criminal career hiding out in that area, robbing banks when he needed the cash. He was killed in a gun battle in Ohio in October, 1934, the hero of outlaws.

The drought was real. And it got worse in 1934 and 1935. The Depression was real. It was not over for several years after this story closes. In fact, some economists say that the event that ended the Depression was World War II.

And finally, those Oklahoma oil wells are real. Oklahoma is one of the leading oil-producing states. Tulsa calls itself the "Oil Capital of the World." If you are interested in doodlebug stories, you might enjoy *The Dickey Bird Was Singing* by Bob Duncan, which I found in the Wichita, Kansas, Public Library. The story of Zeke Proctor is there in more detail.

Oil wells are important. I could not drive my car if there were none around. But how many people do you know who, when they are faced by a good, healthy problem, can go out and find an oil well to solve it?

Sincerely yours,

Ruth Unrau

Contents

Der Herr ist
CLEAN OUT

1
An Oil Well Comes In

Matthew Rempel had one talent that most thirteen year old boys do not have. He could iron white shirts. It was not a talent that he took pride in.

On a Friday afternoon in late April, Matt finished the sixth shirt and slammed his flatiron down on the back of the cookstove. The five Rempel boys and their father each owned one Sunday shirt. After a half day of Matt's effort, all six shirts were now ready for church.

He brushed a tiny fleck of soot off the collar of the shirt belonging to his brother Menno and was immediately sorry. It left a small black streak that Menno would be sure to notice.

"I wonder when Vonnie will be old enough to iron shirts," Matt muttered. "This is no job for a man."

He hung the shirts on a nail in the bedroom and then went to sit on the front steps. He had an hour until milking time. Should he read or go to visit Cornie Berg, his best friend and neighbor to the west?

His answer came in the sound of a Model T clattering down the road. Matt looked up to see Cornie and his brother Karl fly past. Karl must have seen Matt on the front porch, for he braked to a shuddering stop with a bang and an explosion. He backed up like a streak to the Rempel gate and throttled down the motor.

"Jump in," Cornie shouted. "Tolliver No. 1 just came in and we're going over to see her."

Tolliver No. 1 was an oil well four miles south. Matt and everyone else in the community had been waiting to see if it would amount to anything. After a call to his mother, Matt climbed over the door and dropped into the back seat of the open car. Karl took off at twenty miles an hour without a running start. Matt felt as though he'd been left behind, but he had merely been flattened against the seat cushion. A cloud of dust followed them, never quite catching up.

"They say Tolliver No. 1 came in with a gusher as high as the derrick," Cornie shouted above the rattle of the car. "There's oil all over the place."

It was wonderful to be tearing down the dirt road on a pale green afternoon. The noise and the speed and the idea of the oil well made him forget his irritation with those six white shirts. This was as good as being on top of the Ferris wheel.

When they reached the Tolliver farm, they found a crowd already there. Cars of all varieties were parked in the field, from flivvers like Karl's to the latest '32-model black limousines.

The well was not out of control, nor was it spouting over the derrick. The boys got out of the car and joined the jubilant crowd. Everyone seemed to share the Tollivers' elation. The boys pushed their way through to the derrick to learn what they could. There wasn't much to see now. The eighty-foot structure towered over the crowd, casting a criss-cross of shadows in the afternoon sun. The oil company crew was busy laying pipes. A "Christmas tree" valve had been installed over the well, and already oil was flowing into the tanks.

"The Tollivers are sure lucky," Cornie marveled.

"It's hard to see how they deserve it," Matt said. "Old Man Tolliver is about as shiftless as a cowbird."

"Don't step over there, Mrs. Tolliver," a voice called. "You will ruin your shoes in that oil."

Mrs. Tolliver, a woman Matt knew only as Denny Tolliver's mother, looked down over her portly figure at her cracked men's shoes. "What do I care about shoes?" she laughed. "I can throw these away and buy two pair."

A man elbowed Matt aside so he could get closer to Mrs. Tolliver. "I'm from the *Tribune,*" the man said. "Mrs. Tolliver, would you say a word about how it feels to be the owner of a well that looks like a three-thousand-barrel-a-day producer? What will you do with your money?"

Mrs. Tolliver pushed wisps of long hair back into a loose knot and tried to smooth her soiled dress. She drew herself up tall. "I'll feel right at home with money. My family come from England, you know, where they had a castle. We will move to New York, likely, or at least to Tulsy. I'll have to hire me a butler and we will send Dennis to the finest school—"

Before she could give the reporter further details, her tattered husband pulled at her sleeve. "Come on, Maw. We got to get those cows milked, oil or diamonds."

"Hobart Tolliver, don't you tell me to milk no cows. My milkin' days is over. Sell 'em or give 'em away, makes me no matter. From now on I ain't going to look at a cow unless it's in the shape of a T-bone steak."

Mrs. Tolliver departed from the crowd with her head high, as though she were already dressed in silks and satins.

Karl pulled at Matt's arm. "The Tollivers won't ever have to milk another cow, but you boys are not so lucky. Let's move toward the cow pasture."

As they rattled home, slower and more quietly than they had come, Cornie laughed. "Can't you just see Denny Tolliver, molasses on his chin and a safety pin in his shirt, going to a fine school in Tulsy?"

Two miles from the Rempel farm they passed the gray-weathered Crooked Creek schoolhouse where Matt and Cornie just yesterday had spent their last school day.

Matt said, "I guess we won't ever sit at those desks again. Doesn't it make you feel kind of sad to think you are through with school?"

"Not me," Cornie said positively. "I've read my last poem and worked my last problem. I've looked forward to graduating from the eighth grade for nine years. Now I'm a free man."

Matt turned to Karl. "Don't you ever miss school?"

Karl shifted the spark a notch higher to add speed. He shook his head. "I've been out of school for seven years now, and I can't say I ever wanted to go back," he admitted.

Matt did not say more about the subject. None of his family and few of his neighbors had gone past the eighth grade. Matt wanted to go to high school, but he was afraid he would have a hard time convincing Pa that he should attend the high school in Tansy.

Karl stopped the car at the Rempel gate. "See you Sunday," Cornie yelled, and Matt nodded and jumped out. Although the boys did not attend the same church, they always spent their Sunday afternoons together.

Matt grabbed a milk pail off the fence post in the backyard and went to join his brother Waldo at the milking. In nice weather they milked the cows in the open lot back of the barn. Waldo's stocky figure was already folded on the milk stool, his dark head pressed into Rosie's flank. Rosie had to be sung to before she would let down her milk, and Waldo was giving forth with "Dear, dear, what can the matter be?" in his solid baritone.

"Matt, Matt, you are so very late," Waldo sang.

"Yes, yes, milking's a job I hate," Matt vocalized. "I've been to the Tolliver well."

Matt's voice squeaked and Rosie was getting restless, so Waldo had to go back to "Dear, dear," to finish her off. Then, his part of the milking completed, he gave Matt the stool and started for the house with his bucket of milk.

Matt sat down to milk Hardtail. Milking, as well as ironing, was considered woman's work, and Matt disliked it for that reason. Waldo did not seem to mind it. Matt admired the way Waldo went about his work as though he were resigned to doing whatever had to be done. Matt knew that he usually was not thinking of the chore at hand. He was always figuring something out in his mind, how to fix a cultivator or how to make a shortcut in feeding the cattle. Waldo never lost time in fussing about something he could not fix.

Matt wished that he could be more like his sixteen year old brother. Life, according to Matthew, was full of irritations and pleasures, valleys and mountains. He was either at the very top of the Ferris wheel, looking over a perfect world, or he was stopped at the bottom, all the fun ended and nothing to look forward to.

Hardtail gave Matt a swat with her tail that knocked him off his stool and upset his bucket. Matt was about to tell her what he thought of her manners when he heard a mocking laugh from the barn door.

Menno stood there, leaning on his pitchfork, his head thrown back in exaggerated laughter.

"Can't the *Hausfrau* manage the cows tonight?" he taunted in a simpering tone. "Or are your fingers too del-i-cate from housekeeping to do the milking?"

Matt stood up, his anger at Hardtail replaced by rage at his brother. Menno was asking for war by calling him a housewife. Without thinking, Matt charged, throwing his fist at Menno's chin. Somehow, Menno tripped him and Matt found himself on the ground with Menno on top of him, pinning his shoulders to the ground. The wiry Menno had the advantage of five years of muscle over his younger brother, and he knew how to take care of a fighter who was filled more with rage than reason.

"Lemme go, lemme go," Matt panted.

Menno released him. "Got any more fight left in you?"

"Don't you call me a *Hausfrau,* you slick-haired dude."

Menno stood up and smoothed his black hair with a small pocket comb. Matt looked at him with scorn. Menno refused to wear bib overalls as every other farm boy did. He insisted on work pants made like his Sunday suit, with a belt. There he stood, looking like a dandy even in his work clothes.

Matt was so infuriated that he grabbed at Menno's knees and threw him over. Menno was taken off guard and went sprawling in the dust. Matt did not wait for Menno's next move, but jumped up and flew toward the house.

"Come back and fight, you coward," Menno shouted after him.

But Matt had had enough of fighting. In fact, he wondered how he had ever got involved, for he hated fighting. He tangled with his brothers only when they goaded him past common sense. He was afraid that Menno was right —that he really was a coward.

As he went about straining the milk and pouring it into the bowl of the separator, Matt wondered why he had let loose his anger tonight. Menno had been teasing him for three months about his housework. Matt had been ironing shirts and helping with the washing since his oldest sister Mary had come home from Tulsa to tell Esther about a glorious opportunity.

"The Fowlers have friends who would like to hire a Mennonite girl to be nursemaid for their two little boys. Esther, would you like the job? This will just be temporary until Mrs. Hadley gets over her operation."

Matt had watched Esther's face brighten, not realizing that her pleasure would be his affliction.

"Oh, could I?" she appealed to her father. "But I guess I couldn't leave Mama with all the work for you and the boys."

Pa had looked around the table at his eight children and said, "Lester is working at the Springers and I need

Menno and Waldo to help with the farming. Vonnie and John Paul are too little. Matthew, you are the one to stay in and do the heavy work for Mama."

Esther had gone off to Tulsa and Matt had learned to wash, scrub, iron, and even cook a little. He was willing enough to help his mother. She had been ill last year with diphtheria and still tired easily. But he did not enjoy being teased about doing woman's work.

Matt started turning the handle of the cream separator, straining with his muscles until he had the cream pouring from the spout in a steady stream. He liked using his muscles, but not for fighting. He would have to find some other way of getting even with Menno.

Later that evening when the younger ones were in bed, the older brothers and their parents sat around the kitchen table cracking pecans and eating popcorn. They discussed the day in Low German, the language used within the family circle.

DE LAVAL
48 TO 52 TURNS
41
Der Bote
VONNIE
REMPEL
Jan Gleysteen

"What happened to your cheek?" Pa demanded of Menno.

Menno put his hand to his face to finger a bruise that Matt had not noticed before. "Oh, I guess old Hardtail hit me," Menno said.

Matt knew that he had put that bruise there, but he was confident that Menno would not tell on him. If Pa knew they had been fighting, he would wallop them both, old as they were. Pa maintained that Mennonites did not fight. They didn't go to war at home or abroad.

Conversation turned to Tolliver No. 1. Matt gave a first-hand account of the well and the Tollivers' plans.

"Where's the next place they will drill, I wonder?" Waldo asked. "I'd like to have a well close enough so I could watch one come in." Waldo would be more interested in the way a well worked than in the oil that came out of it.

"You know what I heard at the sale today?" Pa asked. "Somebody said the Company is interested in Windy John's place. There is an outcrop of rock in his hay meadow. Some educated fellow thinks it might mean oil."

"Windy John's! His land is right next to ours." In his excitement Matt absentmindedly ate the bitter pecan shell rather than the nut.

"I wouldn't get steamed up about it yet," Menno said calmly. "Fellow I talked to says only one out of nine wells drilled ever amounts to anything."

"He was talking about wildcat wells, probably. We know there's oil around here. Look at Tulsy, thirty miles away, and now the Tolliver well just down the road." Matt got up to get a drink from the water bucket.

Pa shifted in his chair to address Matt. "School let out yesterday, didn't it? You had your last day?"

Matt put the dipper back in the bucket. "Yah, we got our report cards this morning. School's out for this year."

Pa looked up sharply. "For this year? Next year you will be home helping on the farm."

"Pa, couldn't I go to high school?"

Mr. Rempel pushed his chair back from the table and stood up. "You should know better than to ask. No high school."

At the risk of Pa's anger, Matt persisted. "Why?"

"There are good reasons. I need you on the farm. Lester is working out, and we need the money he makes. If Menno can find a job, he should work out, too."

"If the Depression would get better, could you hire someone?" Matt asked, thinking not of the Depression but of Tolliver No. 1.

"There is another reason that you know as well as anyone. A Mennonite is better off without schooling. You go to school and first thing you forget the church, you forget the farm, and you forget the German. No high school."

Pa went into the front room. Matt heard the bed creak as his father sat down. He heard his father's shoes drop to the floor, one and then the other.

No one spoke.

Mama got up from the table and moved over to the sink with the popcorn pan. "It is time for all of us to go to bed."

Matt felt her hand briefly on his shoulder. He moved off with Waldo and Menno to prepare for bed. He moved John Paul from the middle of the bed they shared and crawled in with him. Waldo blew out the butterfly of light in the kerosene lamp and joined Menno in the other double bed.

"Don't take it too bad about Pa," Waldo spoke from the rustle of the straw tick.

"I don't let it bother me any." Matt drew the sheet up tight around his shoulders, pretending drowsiness. He didn't want to hear Waldo's comments, sympathetic or otherwise.

Of course, when you knew Pa, you could see why he acted the way he did sometimes. As a boy, he had come to Canada, by way of Russia, with a group of German Mennonite immigrants. His parents had died of cholera during the crossing and Pa had been left without relatives to make his own way. He had drifted down to Kansas, where he had worked in a Mennonite community as a farmhand. There he had married Helena Enns. After farming in Kansas for five years, he had taken her from the center of a large family to try farming in Oklahoma, where land was cheaper and where he thought he could do better.

Matt could imagine his father as a young man coming to Oklahoma with his lively wife and three small children. He would have looked like Waldo, rather short and stocky; he would have been serious-minded like Lester but with Menno's dash and energy; and he would have had John Paul's stubborn streak. Matt could think of nothing that he had inherited from his father. They were completely unlike, as far as he could see.

Matt knew that Pa had lost one eighty after another in the last five years and that he had only one left, the one they were living on. He was renting the three other eighty acre tracts that he farmed.

Pa had had three years of schooling in Russia in the German Mennonite settlement. He thought that anyone who needed more than eight years must be a *Wirrkopf,* a scatterbrain.

Sometimes Pa spoke too quickly and too loudly on a subject that he had made up his mind about. Having declared himself, he hated to have to change his mind. But much as he hated to admit he was wrong, he had been known to do it.

Pa had once decided that God made horses but not tractors. Therefore, Pa had proclaimed that he would never use a tractor for his farm work. But later, as he came to see the advantages of using a tractor with his large acreage, he had become convinced that God had made men who could invent tractors; and, logically, farmers should use what God provides.

Granted that Pa was honest enough to admit that he could be wrong at times, Matt still had a question in his mind about his father's concern for him. Would his father ever consider the subject of high school worthy of consideration or important enough to weigh the pros and cons? Did he care enough about Matt to try to understand his point of view?

Matt could still hear Pa's last words in his ears, and they were loud and clear and final.

"No high school."

2
A Fight over *Zucka Brucka*

Matt brought the milk to the back porch to strain the next evening; but before he could get the cloth arranged over the milk can, his mother stepped from the kitchen with a large box.

"Your Pa brought a strainer from the farm sale he went to yesterday. Try it. See if you can get the milk a little cleaner." She handed him a funnel with a large bowl and a filter pad about the size of a plate clamped into the bottom.

"I never saw anything wrong with the milk," Matt protested. "The flour sack strains out the mud and the big germs."

"But not the dust and the little germs. Use both the cloth and the filter pad and don't fuss." Mama returned to her kitchen.

The pads were made of a circle of cotton with gauze on each side. Matt was surprised to see how much more dirt the pad strained out. He washed up the milk buckets and then went to clean up for supper at the bench on the back porch.

As he was splashing his face in the basin, a voice said, "Can't you welcome home the prodigal son? I want some fatted calf for supper."

His brother Lester stood before him in his Sunday suit. Mama came through the kitchen door to greet her oldest son and to hear how he had hitched a ride from Prattville. He could stay for the night and the following day, which was Sunday.

The little ones came running, and Pa and the other boys joined the line at the washbasin. They all went in to supper in a gay mood, assuring Lester that if they couldn't give him fatted calf, they could offer pork sausage.

Matt had the feeling, as he bowed his head for grace, that the world was revolving as it should and that some of the members of his family were likable and the others could be tolerated.

After saying grace, Mr. Rempel looked around the table at his children. "It is nice to have you home. I wish Mary and Esther could be here. Maybe next Sunday. Well, help yourself. You don't get your Mama's good cooking every day." He took his own advice and filled his plate with large helpings of fried potatoes and sausage.

"It is good to be back at my own table, Pa," Lester replied.

At twenty, Lester was the oldest boy and Esther's twin. He had been hired out to a Mennonite farmer for a number of years. He said he didn't get homesick anymore, but Matt noticed that he came home every time he could hitch a ride. Lester was the home-loving type.

On the other hand, Menno, although only eighteen, had said that the sooner he could get out on his own, the better he would like it. The first thing he planned to buy was a car. Waldo never expressed a desire either to leave home or to stay. At sixteen he was big and strong enough to work out, but Pa needed him at home.

When he thought about his brothers and sisters, Matt never knew whether he belonged with the older ones or the younger ones. Vonnie and John Paul, ten and seven, were referred to as the "little ones." Matt often felt, to his humiliation, that his parents included him with them.

Lester took a second helping of sausage and remarked casually, "Mr. Springer came home from town this afternoon and said the Prattville Bank had been robbed. They got two thousand dollars."

Menno exclaimed, "Man, if a bank don't go broke, it gets robbed!"

"Who did it? Pretty Boy Floyd?" Matt asked.

"They don't know for sure, but Mr. Springer said they acted just like Floyd's gang."

"How many bank robberies does that make for this part of Oklahoma?" Waldo asked.

Pa said, "It's the Depression. There are bank robberies all over the country. We have more around here because they have the Cookson Hills and the Wildhorse Mountains to run and hide in."

Mama remarked, "Wasn't Pretty Boy Floyd born in the Cookson Hills?"

Matt, who tried to keep up with these things through the *Tulsa Tribune*, answered, "At Salisaw."

"Some say he has killed eight men, counting the sheriff at Bixby two weeks ago," Menno reminded them.

"The *Oklahoma City Star* said that reports were that he

was in China, and then they hear he is out in Hollywood making a picture." Lester got to read the *Star* at the Springers'.

"I say he is hiding out in the Cookson Hills," Pa said with authority. "Pass the *Zwieback.*" He took one of the double buns that Mama baked every Saturday and dunked it in his coffee as the finishing touch to his meal.

Matt took three and crumbled them in a bowl, adding milk and sugar.

"Are you still eating *Zucka Brucka?*" Menno chided. "Baby food!"

Inwardly Matt fumed. Menno was always calling attention to something like this to embarrass him. But he wasn't going to get into a fight in front of Pa. "It's nourishing. Try some," he offered with apparent graciousness.

Lester said, "I believe I will. The Springers never make *Zwieback,*" and he reached for the little two-piece rolls.

Zucka Brucka was not mentioned again until everyone was getting ready for bed. Then Menno, who couldn't stand to have anyone touch his own carefully combed head, tousled Matt's hair and said, "Well, Matty, you had better eat your dish of *Zucka Brucka* and go to bed."

To be called Matty was an insult. He knew a silly girl at school named Matty. To be teased about his bread soup twice in the same evening was asking for war again.

Matt thought about his battle strategy all the while as he took his bath and washed his hair. As he was smoothing down his wet waves at the kitchen sink, he overheard a conversation that suggested a perfect vengeance.

"Did you have Matt use those strainer pads tonight?" Pa asked Mama.

"Yah, the milk is much cleaner."

Matt chose his weapon at that moment and went to bed planning his revenge.

He awoke later than he usually did on Sunday mornings. He dressed quickly, tantalized by the smell of bacon and pancakes. After a hurried washup, he reported to his mother that he would help her with the breakfast.

"Ah, sleepyhead," his mother chided. "Menno said to let you sleep since he could help with the milking."

One thing you could say for Menno, he wasn't lazy. Just mean and ornery. As he went about setting the table, Matt felt almost ashamed of the plan he had for Menno's come-uppance.

He lost his feeling of guilt when Menno came in for breakfast. He ruffled Matt's hair and asked, "How's our *Hausfrau* this morning?"

Matt said quietly to his mother, "Here, you sit down and I will make the pancakes. I will fix the next one for Menno."

Matt had often made pancakes for the family, and they were used to seeing him around the stove. When he was sure Menno was not watching him, he poured some batter into the griddle and then carefully laid a filter pad into it, covering the pad with another layer of batter. After it had baked on one side, he flipped the pancake carefully. It looked perfect.

"Here's your griddle cake," Matt said, placing the plate before his brother.

"That looks good. Let me at it." Menno spread the pan-cake generously with butter and honey.

Then he tried to cut it with his fork. The fork would not

SOMERSE
COUNTY
MAPLE
SYRU

cut through it. Menno looked around the table at the rest of the family, who were eating large forkfuls of pancake and enjoying them. He picked up his knife and tried again.

"Something seems to be wrong with this pancake. Did you let it fry too long?" Menno glanced suspiciously at Matt. His brother, still at the stove frying more pancakes, raised his eyebrows in surprise at such a question.

"He did it just right," Mama defended him. "These are good pancakes."

Menno finally got a piece pulled off and put it in his mouth. He chewed once or twice and then stopped, his cheeks bulging. "It kind of wads up," he said thickly. Then he transferred the mouthful back to his plate.

"This tastes like cotton!" He looked closely at the bite he had been chewing. "It is cotton. Matthew Rempel, did you put cotton in my pancake?"

Menno sprang from the table, ready for the counter-attack, but Matt was too quick for him. He retreated from the battlefield by ducking under the table where the feet of the rest of the family closed a circle around him.

"Come out and fight, you *Taugenichts!*" Menno might consider him a "worth-nothing," but Matt thought he heard a note of grudging respect in his tone.

"I'll make you a good one," he promised as he crawled from under the table, "but that's because you did the milking for me. Just remember: some people like *Zucka Brucka* and some people like cotton pancakes."

"If you're so smart, why aren't you rich?" Menno said.

Matt considered this a pretty weak and unoriginal retort. *"Glummskopp,"* he countered, also without originality, implying that his brother had brains of cottage cheese.

"I think you two are even," Lester refereed.

The taste of victory was sweet as pancake syrup to Matt. This was better than winning a fight with his fists. Or did he feel that way because he was afraid to fight?

"Time to get ready for church," Pa declared after breakfast and devotions. "We don't want to be late."

The family was dressed and sitting on the front porch an hour before it was time to go to church. The boys were in the white shirts that Matt had ironed, and the three older boys were wearing their white duck trousers and white shoes for the first time this season. Matt was not concerned enough about fashion to want a pair of white ducks, and he wore his dark wool trousers without complaint. John Paul had on the knickerbockers that Matt had outgrown. They fastened at the knees over his black stockings. But John Paul would not look fully dressed until his two front teeth grew in.

Vonnie's black hair was smoothly braided for the moment, and her cheeks were rosy from the exertion of having had her hair combed.

Mama stepped out on the porch to sit in the rocker until Lester would bring the car around. It was the only time of the week when Matt saw her without work in her hands. She took pride in seeing her children neatly dressed. Matt had often heard her say to one or the other in her rare English, "Comb your hair. I don't want my family known as the rumpled Rempels." She herself was small and spare with her black hair pulled tight and tidy in its scanty bun.

A strange car came down the road and turned in at the gate, honking all the while.

"Who is that? I don't recognize that horn," Lester said.

They all left the porch to go to see who the stranger was. The visitor, Bill Jantz, was not strange, for he was Lester's best friend. Only the horn was strange. Bill had a new, bright blue 1932 car. Vonnie and John Paul were already standing on the running board.

"It's a Chevrolet convertible cabriolet. See that lid in the back? Lift it up," Bill ordered proudly.

Matt lifted, and the lid opened up to form the back of a seat large enough for two people.

"Boy oh boy oh boy, what a keen car!" Menno exclaimed, his eyes bright with admiration. "What I wouldn't give for a car like that. Isn't it a beaut, Ma?"

"It's a real pretty color," Mama conceded.

"Those wire wheels—did they cost extra?" Lester asked.

"A little. Fifteen dollars for the wheels and fender wells. The whole deal came to around six hundred dollars, but I figure I can make the payments easy when I start harvesting."

"Syno-Mesh and Free Wheeling," Waldo breathed reverently, peering into its less beautiful parts. "I'll bet she rides like a Packard."

"Don't you all want to go for a ride?" Bill offered.

Three at a time, he took everybody a mile up the road and back. "It's like a Ferris wheel," Vonnie said as she stepped up onto the back fender and into the rumble seat. "I'm a little scared."

Everybody agreed that the roadster gave a fine ride. "It took those ruts as smooth as velvet," Menno observed. "I'm going to have a car even if I have to beg, borrow, or steal one."

"It has six cylinders and it gets over twenty miles to the gallon," Bill added to its other merits.

"Did you know," said Vonnie, who read and remembered all the jokes in the *Tulsa Tribune,* "that Columbus got over two thousand miles on a galleon?"

Matt and his brothers groaned, but the joke was lost on John Paul.

"Man, what kind of car did he have?" The little boy put his foot on the running board in imitation of Bill. "Must have been one of those little midgets like an Austin."

"It is too bad that Mary and Esther aren't home," Mama said. "They would have enjoyed the ride." She smoothed the plush brown seat with her hand.

"If they are nice to me, I'll let them have a ride next week," Bill promised. The girls got every other Sunday off from their jobs in Tulsa. "Well, I should get to church. Les, do you want to come with me? And I could take Vonnie and John Paul in the rumble seat."

They took their places in the car and Bill stepped on the starter. "Look, no crank," he grinned.

The rest of the Rempels waved him off and then climbed into their old Model T for the trip to church. Menno said to Matt as they drove out of the yard, "You just wait. Someday I'll have me a car like that."

Matt only nodded. He could appreciate a nice car, but there were other things he wanted more.

3
A Visit to Windy John

A month later on another Sunday, Matt sat in the May sunshine on the steps of the Zion Mennonite Church. He had ridden John Paul's pony, Beauty, over early because it was his turn to unlock the door and sweep out the building.

Matt watched a cloud of dust chase a speeding Model T touring car down the section road. The driver slowed at the gate of the churchyard. The cloud of dust caught up with the car and seemed about to envelop it. But the driver made a sharp turn into the yard, and the pursuing cloud, outwitted, drifted on.

The Model T screeched to a sliding stop beside the other cars. Nine people of varying ages, most of them dressed in white, exploded like popcorn over the sides and through the doors. Matt's family had arrived at church.

His older sisters, Mary and Esther, walked up the steps with Vonnie between them. The girls were home for Sunday from their jobs in Tulsa, and Vonnie followed them around like a kitten. All three were very proper with their eyes straight ahead. Mary and Esther had not a glance for the boys who were leaning against the railing on either side.

Matthew could not understand why his older sisters pretended that the neighbor boys were strangers to them on Sunday morning. They had known these boys most of their lives, but they passed into the church without so much as a greeting.

"Your sister tongue-tied?" Bill Jantz asked Lester.

"You should know. Didn't you bring Mary back from Tulsy last night?" Lester responded.

The other boys hooted and Bill's new tan reddened.

One of their neighbors said, "Bill says he thinks both those Rempel girls are *schmuck.* I wonder how he decided which one to ask."

Matt had never thought that his sisters were good-looking. Mary, twenty-one and lively as a robin, wore her dark hair drawn back in a bun. Esther, Lester's twin, had, like her brother, a more serious expression. She wore her braids in a wreath around her head. Well, if those boys wanted to think his sisters were pretty, it was their business. He didn't care how girls looked.

The church bell clanged. All the boys moved reluctantly through the door. With much scuffling and whispering, they took their places in the back benches on the men's side of the church.

Two hours later, when Sunday school and church were over, the boys bolted out into the violent noon sun as though released from a trap. The older boys stood around the parked cars and discussed the fine points of every car from the Rempels' 1925 Model T to Bill Jantz's 1932 Chevrolet. After the strain of listening to the High German sermon, it was easy to lapse into country-school English.

Matt sat on the running board of one of the cars to listen to the talk. Parents drifted out from the church, reluctant to cut off their visiting, but hungry for their Sunday dinners.

Lester said to Bill Jantz, "Ma told me to tell you to come home with us for dinner."

Matt saw Bill grin and wink at Lester. "Your ma asked me, hey? Well, tell your ma I'll be glad to come. You want to ride home in my car? Might as well ask your sisters if they would care to come with us."

Later at the dinner table, Pa was obviously pleased to have all the family home.

Esther was planning to quit her job with the Hadleys in another month and come home to help her mother. Matt knew he would be as happy as his mother to have her home again. Perhaps he would hear less talk of "woman's work" then. He yearned to get out on the plow or the hayrack.

"I like this job," Esther was saying. "They use crystal thin as air; it will crack if you breathe on it, but I washed the whole set without breaking a piece. And the Oriental rug in the parlor makes me feel as though I was walking on chickweed."

"Don't get any fancy ideas," Lester warned his twin. "I don't know any man around here who would buy you an Oriental rug."

The conversation turned to politics. "I have always favored the Republican ticket," Mr. Rempel declared, "but now I don't know. Times keep getting worse, price of cattle and wheat goes down and down. What are we going to do? Maybe a Democrat could do better."

"Some people think we should recognize the Soviet Union so they could buy our wheat and raise the price," Lester offered. "Mr. Springer says—"

Pa shook his head. "I don't know about those Russians. What do you think, Bill?"

Bill Jantz's pleasant round face took on a serious expression. "I have made up my mind, but I haven't told anybody about it yet. I am leaving Oklahoma."

Forks clattered as the Rempels were caught by surprise.

"Leave Oklahoma!" Lester exploded in disbelief.

"Bill, you clown," Mary said. "You are kidding."

"Are you going to Russia?" John Paul asked.

Bill shook his head. "I plan to go to California. My cousin out there says he can get me a job in his creamery, and I wrote and said to hold it, I'm comin'."

Matt listened for a while to the discussion of hard times and California, and then he started for Cornie Berg's place. He slipped into the narrow woods across the road from the Rempel farm. The woods, little more than a thicket of pecan and blackjack oak, ran along the creek. Matt had discarded his everyday shoes late in April when school was out, and now he rolled up his overall legs to mid-calf and waded across Crooked Creek where it was narrow and shallow. He noted that it was not really deep enough to try to swim in anymore. He wondered when the spring rains would come.

My, but May was a pretty month! The brownish-purple flowers of the pawpaw thickets were still in evidence, although the trees were now leafing out. The leaves of the pecan trees were large and fresh looking, and the grass in the woods was big enough to cover last fall's leaves and brush.

He left the woods to run through the pasture. Along the edge he spotted the bloom of the wild onion and wondered if this was what made the cows' milk taste so disagreeable.

Unexpectedly he came across a patch of prickly pear cactus. In his hurry, he found himself in the middle of it before he could avoid the sharp pricks, and he jumped across it in a startled leap. He turned back then to examine the blossoms. Never before had he seen such a large patch in bloom; the waxy flowers were yellow, some with purplish-red centers, and they looked delicate and mislaid on the prickly cactus stem.

"I've heard said that thriving cactus foretells a dry summer. Or is it that a dry summer brings on the prickly pear?" he mused.

He straightened quickly and started to run again, now through a field of wheat that was knee high and blossoming, and then through a hay meadow. He came to the back of the Berg farmyard. He could see that Cornie was waiting for him in the driveway of the big barn. Matt waved to his friend before he was within hailing distance.

Cornie had many advantages that Matt did not have. He was taller by three inches, although the two boys were about the same age. He had a pleasant face with sandy hair that slicked back neatly when he wanted it to.

Matt thought of himself as ordinary looking. His dark hair was unruly, even curly in damp weather. His sisters sometimes asked him why he looked so serious, and he would be surprised at the question because he was not even feeling serious.

Most of all, Matt envied Cornie's easy way with people. Matt often felt as awkward with his tongue as he was with his feet, and whenever he got up the courage to say something, he seemed to blurt it out.

"Hurry up," Cornie called. "I been waitin'."

Matt ran and arrived breathless at the barn.

"I got a plan," Cornie said.

"Well, tell me." Matt dropped down on a bale of hay to remove a cactus thorn from his dusty foot.

"Let's go over to see Windy John's oil well."

"O. K. Do you think he'll run us off if we trespass in his meadow?"

"He won't be home. A fella like that likes to visit around town on Sundays."

Matt followed Cornie out of the barn and onto the road.

Cornie said, "Did you know about the bank robbery in Hanover? They got away with three thousand dollars."

"Seems like a bank gets robbed every other day," Matt said, and then felt compelled to tell something newsworthy. "Did you know that Bill Jantz is going to California? We will sure miss him. He's always at our house visiting with Lester."

"I hear it is more like visiting with Mary," Cornie said with a smirk.

Matt was taken aback by this idea, but he couldn't appear to accept it. "No, he doesn't care about her. Oh, he does her a favor and takes her to Tulsa on Sunday nights sometimes. He really comes to see Les," Matt insisted.

They were walking back toward Rempels' on the section road. The dust was fine and thick, and they stirred up little clouds of it as they trotted down the road. They crawled through the strands of barbed wire to enter Windy John's meadow. The boys topped a rise in the meadow, and when Matt raised his eyes, he saw the oil well.

The derrick stood outlined against the midafternoon sky, a black network of steel, a windmill without a wheel.

There wasn't much to see actually when they got to the site. A hole had been dug about six feet deep, and cement footings held the four legs of the derrick. When they stood inside the enclosure, they found that it was about twenty feet square, and the derrick rose about seventy feet above them. Steel and lumber were lying there ready for the crew to resume work. The prairie hay had been trampled from the activity of the workers, trucks, and wagons.

The boys threw themselves down on their stomachs in the flattened grass.

"Wouldn't that be a miracle?" Cornie spoke with awe. "To find oil around here. Just think of oil derricks scattered around on our farm the way they are around Tulsy."

"Or around Oklahoma City," added Matt. "Teacher said they have oil wells right by the steps of the Capitol."

Cornie rolled over on his back and stared up into the bright sky and spoke as though he were staring into as bright a future. "I know what I would do if we got oil on our farm. I would buy a palomino and a tooled saddle and fifty-dollar cowboy boots and a real Stetson hat."

Matt said, "And I would buy a brand new 1932 Packard—"

Cornie cut in. "Might as well wait for the next model so it would be brander new." And then he sat upright and laughed aloud. "Did you ever hear about the fella who struck oil and went to town to buy the biggest and best

car he could find and the dealer sold him a hearse?"

"Sure, that's an old one." Matt was glad that he could top that joke. "Like the Indian who struck oil and bought a new car every time he had a flat tire. Just left the old one to sit by the side of the road."

Cornie turned to Matt. "Don't you want nothing besides a Packard? Everything's free today, you know."

Matt was quiet for a moment and then he said, "There is something I want more than a Packard, but I don't know if even an oil well would get it for me."

Cornie whistled. "Man, what do you want that is so expensive? The moon?"

Matt shook his head. "I want to go to high school."

Cornie hooted. "Why would you want that, for land's sake? Be glad you don't have to go to school." Cornie eyed him suspiciously. "You ain't planning to be a teacher, are you?"

Matt, who had admired every teacher he had had, nevertheless protested, "Of course not. I mean I don't know. I just *want* to go to school because I want to learn something. But Pa thinks it would be a waste of time and money."

"Don't be so gloomy. You're better off at home. You would just get worldly ideas and the church would put you out."

Matt nodded. "Pa says that if I would get educated I wouldn't be a good Mennonite."

This theological discussion was interrupted by an approaching figure.

Cornie said softly, "Hey, here comes Windy John. Do you think he is mad?"

Windy John Boston was a familiar figure, but he was not really well known to Matt. His farm adjoined the Rempel eighty, but it was cut off from view by a rise of meadow. Matt knew that his father and Windy John did some neighboring, exchanging tools and help occasionally. Matt was a little frightened of the man, for he had a reputation for being silent and gruff.

Windy John's appearance was not reassuring. In the first place, he had a peg leg on which he could maneuver as well as anybody with two good legs. He had fastened a tin can to his peg to protect its tip, and it gleamed below his overall cuff. And then he was a large man with a shock of grizzled hair.

"Hello, Mr. Boston," Cornie called politely as Windy John approached. "We were just admiring your derrick."

The old man stopped in front of them. "You boys ain't smokin', are you?" he asked suspiciously. "I don't want no fires around here."

"No, sir. We was just talking about oil," Cornie assured him.

Windy John regarded them silently for a moment, and Matt wondered if he was going to order them off. Then he lowered himself to the ground and carefully crossed his wooden leg over his good one.

"What do you boys think of my oil well?" His speech was slower and had more of a Southern drawl than his Oklahoma neighbors.

"What made the Company pick this spot?" Matt asked.

"Well, first a geologist fella comes around and takes a look at the land and putters around making tests." Windy John ran his fingers through his thatch of gray hair. "And then a fella comes who says he is a seismologist and he pokes around with dynamite and starts a pint-sized earthquake here and there, and one of his gadgets says there might be oil around here."

Matt was surprised to find that Windy John could make a speech. His father had always said that his neighbor was as close-mouthed as a turkey egg.

"But why did they come to your farm instead of one of ours?" Cornie asked. Matt was interested in that question, too.

A little smile played at the corners of Windy John's eyes. "I'll tell you. Down in Texas once I puttered around locatin' oil wells and kind of got the hang of it. I told the

Company I thought there was oil here, and they got interested."

"Gee, Mr. Boston, how do you find an oil well?" Cornie asked.

"You boys won't want to believe this, educated as you are, but I find my oil wells with a peach branch."

Cornie sat straight up. "You mean you're a water witch who can find oil?"

"You might call me that. I'm the seventh son of a seventh son, which some people say gives me special powers. Other people call me a doodlebug."

Cornie turned to Matt. "Remember old Grote Nekkel? He was the seventh son of a seventh son and he knew that the world was coming to an end on July 12, 1931."

"It happened he was wrong," Matt offered, perhaps unnecessarily. "Did the Company believe you, Mr. Boston?"

"They sent Mr. Fenwig out and he got excited and give me a lease for the oil rights, and now they are goin' to find out how good they guessed."

"Golly, Mr. Boston, you mean it's only guesswork?" Matt demanded.

"With the seismologist, it's guesswork about half the time. With me, no. My peach branch is always right."

The boys looked at Windy John with new respect. "Mr. Boston, what do you aim to do with the money you make from your oil well?" Cornie asked.

"Well, now," Windy John looked thoughtful and his drawl stretched his words out like the rubber band in a slingshot. "Well, now, I thought maybe I would buy me a new saw. My old one won't take an edge no more."

Matt saw the twinkle in the old man's eye and said,

"Oh, you're making *Schputt.* You'll probably build you a fine big house in Tulsy and live easy."

"Livin' in Tulsy ain't to my taste," Windy John declared. "I been a pea-patch farmer for so many years, I reckon I'm too old to change."

"How did you learn so much about oil?" Matt asked.

"I always lived in oil country. Had a little well of my own in Texas, but I sold out and bought this little place a few years ago. Long time ago when I was a young man, I used to be a roughneck."

"A roughneck? You mean a tough guy?" Cornie asked.

Windy John shook his head. "No, no. I mean I worked for a drillin' crew. But it was a rough life, and dangerous, too, back in the old days."

"Is that how you lost your leg?" Cornie asked the question that Matt was too timid to mention.

Windy John's expression changed. "I usually tell little tykes who ask that I got it caught in a Texas rabbit hole."

"We are not little tykes," Matt said.

"I lost my leg in the war. It was blown off by a grenade, almost fifteen years ago. But you boys wouldn't understand about that, bein' Mennonites and objectors to war. You wouldn't understand that even though I was over the age they wanted, I volunteered to fight. And you wouldn't understand how it feels to lose your leg for nothin' two days after the Armistice was signed."

Both boys were silent. Matt heard a bitterness in John Boston's voice that he could not speak to. What was there to say? He knew that he didn't understand, but he could sense something of the anguish that the old man evidently still felt.

"Well, it's not your fault you was born of a stock that lacks courage," Windy John said. Then his tone softened. "Here, give me a hand up. It must be time for you boys to go home and do your chores."

They all rose and started back toward the road, Windy John keeping up with long, slow steps.

As they approached the farmyard, Matt saw a figure slip around the corner of John's shack of a house and disappear through the door.

"Who's that, Mr. Boston?" Cornie asked. "I thought you lived here alone."

Windy John seemed to lose his friendliness. "That's just my nephew."

"What's his name?" Cornie persisted, his curiosity getting the better of his good manners.

"His name? Why his name is Charlie. Yes, his name is Charlie—Boston. Now you kids hike home. Don't go back to that well without my say-so, hear me?"

They hiked. When they were out of earshot, they wondered.

"I wonder why Windy John lost his breeze when we saw that nephew," Matt wondered. "Was he hiding him?"

"I wonder why Charlie didn't come over and say hello to us," Cornie wondered.

"Did you know that Pretty Boy Floyd has a first name of Charles?"

Cornie didn't, and the fact didn't interest him very much. At the corner they parted, reluctant for the day to end but knowing that they were going to be late for chores.

4
Matt Helps with Threshing

Matt looked forward to threshing. His father had halfway promised him that he could do a man's work on the threshing crew this year.

"What can a little punkin like you do?" his older brothers had joked. "Pitching bundles into the threshing machine, that is man's work."

"I am big for my age." That was stretching it a little, he knew. "I could watch the grain wagons. It's time I graduated from water boy. Even John Paul is big enough to be water boy."

Although oil was considered the black gold of the Oklahoma prairies, the real gold was the wheat, according to the old-timers. In spite of the dry spring, the wheat of this year was fairly good, for it had got a good start.

This was the dinner-table conversation, and Mr. Rempel grumbled that he should have planted more wheat instead of so much oats, which had not done so well. But, on the other hand, wheat wasn't bringing a good price, either.

There was to be only one day for threshing wheat this year. Mama was not worried about getting the dinner.

Esther was home now for the summer so that she could help her mother with the heavy work of cooking for threshers and hayers and later with the canning of garden stuff. Esther had been full of ideas about maids and chauffeurs, fancy foods and fancy clothes. But she soon had readjusted herself to farm life and went about cooking and cleaning and milking cows with her usual good humor.

The threshers were expected at the Rempel farm on Wednesday, but on the preceding Monday afternoon, a message came from the Voths saying that Mama's Aunt Annie had died suddenly in Kansas. The funeral was to be on Wednesday.

Mama must go to the funeral. Mr. Rempel would have it no other way. The Voths were related to Aunt Annie's husband. Some of the Voths would be driving to the funeral, and Mama could ride with them.

Mama didn't see how it would be possible for her to go, with threshers coming, but Pa pointed out that Esther was home and she and Vonnie could manage. Mama hadn't been back to Kansas for three years, and this was a good chance for her to see her family.

So Mama flew to work yet Monday evening and baked five pies, emptying cans of peaches, apples, and cherries for filling. She and Esther also baked a mountain of bread and *Zwieback,* white, brown, and rye. Matt went to sleep Monday night hungry from the smell of baking.

Mama left early Tuesday morning, feeling a little guilty, she said, to be looking forward to going to Kansas when the occasion was so sad; and feeling even more guilty because she was leaving the family at such a busy time.

She wore her dark blue dress with its white lace collar

and gold pin, and her black hair was pinned on top of her head in its usual skimpy bun. Pa said he wished she had had time to buy a new dress to wear among her Kansas relatives.

"Ach waut, the relatives won't know this isn't a new dress," she consoled him.

Matt silently doubted this. Even he was aware that it was not made anything like his older sisters' dresses.

After she had gone, Pa decided to go to town for ice so the pies could be kept cool. Esther set about cleaning the ice chest in the summer kitchen, and she gave Matt the task of churning butter. He knew that it had to be done, for they needed plenty of fresh butter for threshers, but he hated the job worse than almost anything else he was asked to do around the house, almost as much as ironing shirts.

He sat down on the edge of the front porch, letting his legs dangle to the ground, and started the dasher thumping. It was comfortable here in the morning shade, but the sun was already blazing. A half-mile away toward the north he noticed the dust of a speeding car driving with the top down. Who would drive with the top down in this sun? The big black car came back and turned down the road that led past the Rempel house. It turned in at the gate and stopped in front of Matt with a screech of brakes.

"Is this the Rempel place?" a tired voice asked.

"Yes," Matt answered, not missing a thump in his churning as he looked over the beautiful car.

"Esther Rempel live here?"

"Yes."

Matt kept churning, lifting the dasher up and down automatically. The car was a 1932 Packard convertible!

"Why doesn't she live where people can find her? I have spent an hour driving up and down these blasted dusty desert alleys."

A layer of dust covered not only the fenders and hood and trunk, but also the fine cushions.

The man at the wheel was getting impatient. "Could you ask Miss Esther to come here?"

Matt shifted his eyes from the car to look at its driver, a youngish man who was dressed in a once-white suit.

Matt dropped the churn dasher with a polite, "Yes, sir," and ran back to the summer kitchen to tell Esther.

"There is a Packard here to see you. I mean, a man dressed in a white Packard wants you to come out."

Esther was puzzled. "That sounds like Mr. Hadley. My goodness, what does he want? He knows I can't work for him until August. See if you can find my shoes."

She made sure that her crown of brown braids was tidy, put on her shoes, and stepped out like a princess in her flour-sack apron to greet Mr. Hadley.

Her former employer had come from Tulsa that morning at the command of his wife. He was to bring Esther back with him. The Hadley family was going to Eureka Springs in Arkansas for a week's vacation, and Mrs. Hadley refused to go unless Esther would come along to take care of the children.

"Eureka Springs," Esther breathed. "I have always wanted to go to Eureka Springs."

"Fine, go pack your suitcase. I'll just get me a drink from the well here." Mr. Hadley started to pump vigorously but without results.

Matt's first thought was, "That will be great for Esther.

I wonder how I could make them ask me," and then he was struck with horror.

"You can't go!" he exploded.

Esther stopped in the doorway, and Mr. Hadley stopped pumping to swing around to face him.

"Why not?" they asked in unison.

At that moment the water gushed from the pump spout and flooded the dust off Mr. Hadley's white shoes. It also splashed mud on his white pants.

"It takes a minute for the pump to get started," Matt observed for Mr. Hadley's information. Mr. Hadley tried to wipe off his wet trouser cuffs with his white handerchief.

The Model T drove into the yard and parked beside the Packard. Mr. Rempel descended and shook hands with Mr. Hadley, and Esther told Pa about this opportunity to go to Eureka Springs.

Pa shook his head. "The threshers. Should they go hungry so that you can go gallivanting to Eureka Springs?"

Esther drooped with disappointment. "For a moment I had forgotten about the threshers."

"She will be getting full pay for a nice vacation," Mr. Hadley reminded them.

Matt felt his father's eyes upon him, and he took his own eyes from the gleaming headlights of the Packard to see that his father had a speculative look. And then with shock he read his father's mind.

"I can't cook a thresher dinner!" Matt protested.

Mr. Rempel nodded to himself. "I believe Matt could do it. He is very handy in the kitchen, and Vonnie could help him. Go pack your suitcase, Esther. We can make good use of your wages. Let me fix you a drink of ice water, Mr. Hadley."

Matt went back to his churn, feeling doubly humiliated. Here he was, just a little kid and expected to cook a whole thresher dinner. He knew he could never do it. Why, he didn't know any more than John Paul did about cooking for threshers. It just went to show that Pa cared more about all the other children than he did about Matt.

Esther could not desert him like this. But she did. Mr. Hadley dusted off a place for her on the front seat and they roared away toward Tulsa.

After they had gone Pa said, "Take care of the butter and then start tomorrow's dinner. I'd like to help, but I don't know much about the kitchen."

Matt knew that his father was right about that. His mother had said more than once that Pa hardly knew enough about a kitchen to butter his own bread.

Matt looked at the kitchen clock and saw that it was almost eleven. Another horror struck him. Who was to cook for the family while Mama and Esther were gone? Well, when they got tired of eggs and fried potatoes, they could do the cooking themselves, he decided.

For dinner they had an ordinary meal of potatoes boiled in their jackets and ham with cream gravy. But for supper Matt decided to try something he knew would please the family.

He made a dough which he rolled out and cut into squares. He spooned a mixture of cottage cheese and onion onto the center and pressed another square of dough on this. He dropped the *Wareneki* into boiling water and cooked them for five minutes.

"You are a good cooker," John Paul complimented him.

Matt was satisfied with that. He was a little deflated when Waldo informed him that he had forgotten to salt the butter. Matt had to unmold it, mix in the salt, and remold it.

"Don't make any mistakes like that when the threshers come," Pa cautioned. "They would go home and tell their wives what a poor cook you are. And be sure to cook plenty of food."

Vonnie said, *"He frat aus een Drascha,"* and laughed.

"Is that a joke?" John Paul asked her.

" 'He eats like a thresher'? Yes, sort of. That's what we say about someone who eats a lot, and here we will have a tableful of threshers eating like threshers."

"It could be a riddle," John Paul suggested. "What eats like a thresher? Answer, a thresher."

"There is no point to it," Vonnie decided. "But it might make a poem. What rhymes with thresher?"

"Fresher," offered Matt. "He eats like a thresher, but a flower smells fresher."

Vonnie would have none of it. "That is not a poetic thought."

After supper Matt sat down with pencil and paper to make out a menu.

Matt read off the menu to the family. "We will have roast beef, boiled potatoes, gravy, canned corn, lettuce, sauerkraut, bread, butter, pie, and iced tea."

On the other side of the table, Pa nodded his approval. "Get everything organized good. That is the way to do it. I guess you learn that at school, yah? I never was good at organizing."

Pa's approval made him feel good, but later when he was trying to fall asleep, all the details of cooking a meal went tumbling through his head, and he knew he could never do it. What if he burned the potatoes or forgot to put the meat in the oven?

Did any other family expect so much of a thirteen-year-old boy?

Matt was wakened before sunup by the cheerful blast of the whistle of the steam engine. That whistle meant that Ben Voth was getting the threshing rig ready to go.

Matt and Vonnie got breakfast out of the way and settled down to potato peeling. Pa came home from Tansy with the beef roast, and they laid it in the big graniteware roaster and shoved it in the oven. They had plenty of time to get the rest of the meal together and set the table. Pa came in every hour to ask how they were getting along.

"I should never have let Esther go. What will we do if there isn't enough or if something burns?" he asked nervously.

"We'll watch it, Pa," Vonnie assured him, and then ran off to play.

About eleven o'clock Matt took a look around and discovered that Vonnie had not done the cleaning. He had to go find her and drag her back. She was out along the road gathering wild flowers for a centerpiece for the table.

"They won't notice that the beds aren't made," she protested when he scolded her.

"Ma would be shamed beyond words if the threshers saw that the beds weren't made," Matt insisted. "Come on."

Matt helped her with the cleaning because he was afraid

she might not get done in time to help with the meal. It didn't take long. The house had only three rooms. There was the front room which served as a parlor and a bedroom for his parents and Vonnie.

The boys' room was off the kitchen. There was no bedroom for the older girls. When they came home, the boys moved into the hayloft or the girls slept on the black leather sofa.

The threshers would eat in the kitchen. It would be cool enough because the big black cookstove had been moved out to the summer kitchen, a separate little building a few yards from the back porch. All the food was prepared out there during the hot months and brought to the kitchen.

The meal was ready to dish up when Matt heard the men coming to the house. It was at this moment that he got nervous hands and weak knees, but he was soon so busy dishing up food and filling glasses with iced tea that he forgot his fears.

Of the men at the table, all were neighbors but not all were well known to Matt. A few of them went to the Zion Church, but there were several Amishmen with their beards and hook-and-eye clothes. Matt saw little of them except on coyote hunts or at threshing and silo filling times. Sometimes he saw them going to church in their buggies, for the Amish thought it wrong to use cars and tractors. Two Holdeman Mennonites were in the threshing ring too. They wore beards as the Amish did, but they could drive cars.

There were also two "English" neighbors, Lutherans who could speak High German better than anyone else at the table. The Mennonites called them *English* because they were not Mennonite or Plautdeutsch. Windy John was there, too. Matt had heard that he was a Baptist.

After the first pangs of hunger had been satisfied, the men started teasing Matt.

"I hear you cooked the dinner," Karl Berg said. "This has been a good appetizer. Now where's the main course?"

"Here, have some pie," Matt said, and put three pies on the table.

"I thought all you could make was *Zucka Brucka,*" Karl ragged him.

Matt felt his good humor slipping and cast a dark look at Menno.

"Don't forget to do the dishes," Menno cautioned as he got up from the table.

But Pa said clearly, "Menno, you stay and help the young ones with the dishes."

"Aw, Pa," Menno protested amid the general laughter, but in vain. He tied on an apron to protect the kitchen from his dirty overalls and washed while Waldo dried. Matt, Vonnie, and John Paul ate at their leisure while the men sprawled out on the front porch to take short naps.

After cleaning up the kitchen, Matt was free to join the threshing crew.

Ben Voth hired an engineer to fire the steam engine and watch the valves to see that the pressure was right. The steam furnished power to run the belt that kept the separator separating the wheat from the straw. Waldo was the water monkey. His job was to see that the boiler of the steam engine was always full.

Mr. Rempel gave Menno and Karl Berg the job of

measuring out one hundred bushels of wheat for the landlord of one of the eighties he rented.

"I know how we could measure the wagon box and figure the number of bushels in the wagon," Matt suggested. "Then you wouldn't have to scoop all of it, only enough to make a hundred bushels even."

Menno had no confidence in such a method. "We'll scoop it into this half-bushel measure and do it right."

But Pa was interested. "You mean there is a way to measure without scooping? I know that our own wagon holds sixty bushels, but this one isn't the same size."

"I'll show you," Matt said, and he ran for a yardstick, a pencil, and a scrap of paper. He measured and multiplied and divided. He announced after a few minutes, "There are one hundred seventy-two bushels in that wagon box."

Meanwhile, Karl and Menno had started scooping and measuring, trying to keep count as they emptied one wagonload of wheat into another, losing track of how many bushels they had scooped, agreeing about it, and making *Schputt* of Matt and his arithmetic.

"Anybody knows this wagon will not hold twice as much as the other one. You can tell by looking. There is just one thing wrong with these educated ideas: they never work," Menno insisted.

Soon there was a shout from Karl, "There, we had seventy bushels in this wagon. He was only off by a hundred and two." He and Menno laughed at Matt's confusion.

Matt went back to his scrap of paper. "Shucks, I made a mistake in addition. Well, anyway, my method was right."

But Menno and Karl were not interested in method.

Windy John drove up with a rackful of grain bundles, and since there were two already ahead of him, he came over to sit in the shade of the barn. Matt joined him. They sat hunkered down with their backs to the barn.

"How are they coming with your oil well, Mr. Boston?"

"It looks like we're about to see some action there. They have the housing built and are about ready to spud in."

"Spud in?"

"They are ready to take the first bite out of the ground and start drillin'. Haven't you ever seen a crew drill for oil?"

"I see those wells pumping whenever we go to Tulsa, and I saw Tolliver No. 1 after it came in, but I've never seen the men do the drilling."

Windy John blew through a straw. "You come over and watch how they do it. They have a bit on the end of a cable, and they keep droppin' this bit till they have a hole punched into the ground."

"Doesn't it take a long time to get far down where the oil is?"

"Oh, yes—three, four months or more. They might have to go a mile down."

Windy John took his little silver pocketknife out and began cutting his grimy fingernails. "I thought you had a mighty fine dinner there today. Do you like to cook?" he asked.

"Well, I have to admit I don't mind it much. But I don't like to be teased about being a *Hausfrau.*"

"Never you mind that. I admire a man who can do a good job of what has to be done, and if its cookin', he should be a good cook. I don't practice what I preach when it comes to my own housekeepin', I have to admit."

If a big man like Windy John didn't see anything wrong with a boy's doing the cooking, Matt guessed he shouldn't feel it was sissified. Menno was just trying to get his goat by teasing him about it.

"That is a pretty little knife," Matt said.

"The only keepsake I have from my mother. She used to carry it around in what she called her reticule."

There was a silence until Matt asked, "Charlie still around?"

"Charlie?"

"Your nephew, Charlie Boston."

"Oh, he comes and goes." With that Windy John got up and went back to the noise and dust of the threshing crew, although there was still one rack before his.

Matt went back to the house to make sandwiches for the men's lunch. Why was Windy John so reluctant to talk about his nephew? Or could it be that his nephew was not his nephew?

The threshing crew worked until seven that evening to finish up the job, and then one by one the wagons headed home to the rattle of harness and the snorts of horses and mules. The steam engine and the separator chugged out of the yard and down the road to the next place.

"This will probably be the last beef we will have for a while," Pa warned as they ate the leftovers that evening. "There isn't cash money to buy meat now. Wheat at forty cents a bushel is hardly worth growing, but I'll have to save most of this crop for seed."

After supper Pa and Waldo went across the road to

Crooked Creek to wash themselves and their dirt-stiff clothes. They put on clean work clothes and hung their dripping wash on the back fence. Waldo complained that there was hardly enough water in Crooked Creek for taking a decent bath.

They lounged around on the front porch for a while then. Pa tried to read *Der Bundesbote* by the fading daylight, grumbling about the hard times.

Suddenly he turned to Matt. "Where did you learn to figure the number of bushels in a wagon box? Is that in the arithmetic book?"

Matt rolled from his back to his stomach so he could look at his father. "That's in the high school arithmetic book, but the teacher let me work in it before school was out."

"I'd rather measure things out the long way than go to school to learn that," Waldo volunteered from his place on the porch step.

"But that's good," Pa insisted. "That's good that you can learn such things. Matt, I think you got a good head."

Was Pa saying that there might be some use for school? Could he be thinking of letting Matt go to high school?

"Pa, there's lots of useful things I could learn from that arithmetic book. Maybe if we had an oil well—" Matt began.

"Listen to the dreamer," Waldo said to the rising moon.

"Don't count on the oil," Pa cautioned. "Mr. Fenwig stopped last week, and he says that the Company isn't in a hurry to put any more wells around here. One of their rock hounds says that there is no oil around here and another says that there is a pool right under our cornfield."

In spite of Pa's tone of caution, Matt's spirits began to rise. He wanted to go to high school, and here was Pa giving him a faint hope that perhaps schooling was good. But to be able to afford to go to school, Matt needed a miracle—like an oil well. Pa had said, "Don't count on the oil," but Matt didn't pay attention. Those last words, "There is a pool right under our cornfield," had a better sound.

"Karl Berg says that the bank at Twister was robbed in the style of Pretty Boy Floyd yesterday. Anything about it in the *Tribune?*" Waldo asked.

"Yah, right here. There is a reward of three thousand dollars for whoever catches him." Matt handed the paper to Waldo.

"They think he is hiding in the Cookson Hills yet." Waldo turned to Matt. "Cookson Hills ain't so far off. Why don't you go find Pretty Boy and collect three thousand dollars? That would keep you in gumdrops for quite a spell."

"Bedtime," Pa commanded, and nobody argued with him, although twilight was just giving way to night.

The boys dragged their straw ticks out on the porch to get the breeze. From his bed Matt could see the white evening primroses floating in the moonlight out along the road. He was glad the day was over, but it was good to feel that he had done something that he thought he couldn't do. How many boys could cook a dinner for a bunch of threshers?

He dreamed that he was serving bowls full of primroses to the threshers. When they asked him what he was feeding them, he replied, "White oil."

5
Charlie Robs a Bank

Mama came home from the funeral in Kansas and Esther came home from her vacation in Eureka Springs. The rest of the family listened to the glories of both places and wished that they could go someplace, anyplace.

"When we get rich, we will all go to the Rocky Mountains in Colorado," Pa promised grandly.

Matt realized that his father was not rich. Nobody was rich that he knew except the Fowlers, where Mary worked. They owned the Fowler Oil Company and never seemed to worry about the Depression. Then there were the Hadleys, Esther's employers. The Hadleys owned acres and acres of prairie and raised blooded cattle. "Gentlemen farmers," Pa called them with a shade of contempt. Everybody in the Tansy community worked hard at farming, and most of them felt lucky just to make a living from the farm.

Probably Banker Schnell was rich. He had the biggest house in Tansy, but of course there were not many big houses in Tansy. Matt wondered about Ben Voth. Was he rich? He owned the threshing rig and had money for trips to California and always had a new car. But that ended the list of rich men that Matt had any knowledge of.

For the truth was that the country was in the Big Depression. This was the third year for it. It had started after the stock market crash in 1929. Pa said that farmers had been in the Depression since 1920. From what Matt read in the paper, he concluded that the whole world was in a bad state, every country suffering from its own Depression and none of them able to help anybody else.

Matt saw hard times in the number of tramps that went through the country, usually following the railroad on their way to California. Sometimes they stopped by the farm to ask for a day's work or a free meal. Pa always gave them food, and sometimes he let them work if he could pay them in food and a bed in the hayloft.

Another mark of the Depression was the number of bank failures. Every issue of the *Tulsa Tribune* named a bank that had "gone under." Mama said uncertainly that maybe they should not put their little money in the Tansy bank. It might fail, too.

But Pa reassured her. "That's why banks fail, because people lose faith. Our Tansy bank is a good one. I know Henry Schnell. He's not a Mennonite, but his folks come from the Old Country, and he is a good man."

Then there were the sales. You could expect older people to retire and sell out to some ambitious young married couple. But many farmers had had their mortgages foreclosed by the banks and *had* to move off. Everything sold cheaply.

Pa came home from a sale one afternoon in July with a variety of bargains. He had bid on some tools and found that a goat was included with the lot. Vonnie took him to her bosom, smelly and selfish as he was, and christened him Donald.

"That is an elegant name and it means 'world ruler,'" she declared. Donald accepted the name.

Also at the sale Pa had picked up for a nickel a box of magazines and books which he turned over to Matt.

"But don't read them when you should be working," his father admonished.

Matt had accepted the box gladly, but he was disappointed to find that it was filled with *Good Housekeeping* magazines and some old textbooks.

Glancing through one of the magazines, though, he was struck by an inspiration.

"Win a free refrigerator," the advertisement read. "Fifty cash prizes of five hundred dollars and a free refrigerator will be given for the best twenty-five words on 'Why I would like to have a Deepfrost refrigerator,' plus hundreds of other prizes."

In that summer of heat and dust, a refrigerator would be the greatest gift he could give to his family, Matt decided. Some things like butter and milk would stay cool if you put them in a bucket and hung them in the well. And when you had to have ice, you bought twenty-five cents' worth for the ice chest. But if they had a refrigerator, the family would eat ice cream, Jello, sodas, lemonade, and everything cold and frosty until they froze their insides. What would it be like, walking around in the sun feeling like a human icicle?

His highest aim was to win the five hundred dollars, of course. For five hundred dollars Pa could hire a man for a year. He might be persuaded to let Matt go to school.

Pa had said not to read when he should be working, and Matt followed the letter of that law. He worked and read at the same time. He read when he plowed the long furrows to break the sod of the east pasture that Pa was putting into wheat. The field was almost a half-mile long, and the mules could follow the furrow easily without his guidance. So Matt read the stories in *Good Housekeeping.* There was a continued story by Peter B. Kyne, and every installment was there. Sometimes the mules, sensing that Matt was paying no attention to them, slowed and stopped. Sometimes he did not realize that they had stopped, and when he awoke from his reading, he wondered guiltily how long they had been resting there in the middle of the field.

Then he would put his magazine down, get the mules started, and think rather than read.

He thought about what he would write in twenty-five words or less about why he liked Deepfrost refrigerators. He would take a stub of pencil and a scrap of paper from his pocket and start writing.

The writing was a more difficult task than he had thought it would be. He had never seen a Deepfrost except in the picture. Nobody he knew had a Deepfrost. Nobody he knew had a refrigerator.

Evenings after supper, Matt studied the advertisement carefully to see what the selling points were. After a week of mulling it over, he decided on this version:

I would like to have the Deepfrost Refrigerator because then for the rest of my life I could have a cool drink any time.

The deadline for sending in the entry was not far away, and he had to get to town to get the entry blank from the Deepfrost dealer. That would be hard to manage, but he thought he could do it.

His first effort was in Tansy.

Tansy was five miles from home and the town where the Rempels did their trading. Mama took her cream and eggs to the Tansy Grocery and Department Store. Pa did his banking at the Tansy State Bank. There were also a garage, a post office, a pool hall, two churches, an elevator, four hundred residents, and one main street, unpaved. But most important to Matt was the Edwards' Furniture Store and Undertaking Parlor.

He went with the family one Saturday night and casually walked into Edwards' store.

When he asked to see the Deepfrost, Mr. Edwards said, "Sorry, son, we don't carry the Deepfrost. All we have in stock are ice chests. Could I show you this Coolair?"

Mr. Edwards looked puzzled, but Matt shook his head and did not explain his request. It was his own business if he wanted to win a refrigerator for his family. Matt thanked him and left the store wondering where in Tansy he would find an entry blank.

Later when the Rempels were gathering at the car to head for home, Mr. Edwards approached them. He poked his head under the car top and leaned his elbows on the door frame.

Matt grew tense. To himself he said, "Is he going to tell Pa that I asked in his store for a Deepfrost?"

But all Mr. Edwards asked was, "You folks about to get electricity at your place, Pete?"

Pa, surprised at such a question, said, "Electricity? Where would it come from? I couldn't afford one of these Delco plants."

Ma, sitting between Pa and Waldo in the front seat, leaned over to ask, "My land, what makes you ask?"

Mr. Edwards shrugged. "Just curious. Goodnight, folks," and then he withdrew his head and wandered back to his store.

Before Waldo could get the car started, Mr. Schnell, the banker, strolled by with his wife on his arm. He paused at the Rempel car. "How are you, Pete, and Helen? Good to see you in town." He spoke in High German.

Mr. Rempel was obviously flattered to be so addressed and he answered in his best German, "Good evening, Henry, Mrs. Schnell. You think this Depression is about over?"

Mr. Schnell pursed his lips thoughtfully. "I sure wish I could say that prosperity is right around the corner, Pete, like the Democrats say, but I think President Hoover needs six months to get Congress moving so this country can get going again. But I have every confidence that he will."

Matt wanted to ask Mr. Schnell his opinion of Mr. Roosevelt, but he didn't have the courage.

His father said, "I hear Roosevelt was defeated in the California primary. Maybe the Democrats will choose Garner; you think so?"

Mr. Schnell gave a disparaging gesture. "Don't you believe it, Pete. Al Smith will get the Democratic nomination, and President Hoover will beat him easily. He has a program started that will pull this country out of the Depression, you wait and see."

Mrs. Schnell was growing impatient. "Nice to talk to you folks. Drop in at the bank any time. Always glad to take your deposit."

"He sure is a nice man," Pa declared as Waldo started the car and backed out. "They don't come any nicer."

"There's been many a nice banker whose bank failed," Mama observed.

"Now, don't you worry about Henry Schnell's bank," Pa said. "It's sound as an oak tree. Henry Schnell is an educated man. Matthew, you want to be educated so you can be a banker like Mr. Schnell?"

"No, Pa. I don't think so."

"It would be a good job. There's always money. Even in a Depression."

Matt rode back home in his own depression of disappointment. How would he ever get a certificate from a Deepfrost dealer? Then his ear picked up a conversation from the front seat between Waldo and his father.

"I heard tonight that they are paying a cent more for wheat over in Wellington," Pa said. "I think I'll send a load over Monday."

"Can we spare a load?" Mama asked. "I thought you said we should save ours for seed wheat."

"I need some cash right now," Pa replied. "I have to pay Ben Voth for the threshing."

Matt spoke up from the back seat. "Pa, can I take the wheat to Wellington?"

"We'll see."

That wasn't a definite answer, but it was all Matt needed to start counting on the trip to Wellington. He would sit high up on the wagon seat, driving those horses like an old mule skinner. Pa always used the horses when he drove to Wellington, for they were a handsome pair. Matt would take that wheat to the elevator like any grown man who had to haul a load of wheat. And when it was weighed and he had the check for it, he would go to the Mercantile Company and look at the Deepfrost.

John Paul drooped and slept on his lap, and Vonnie slept on John Paul, and the three of them leaned on each other like a row of collapsed dominoes until they arrived home.

The trip to Wellington worked out almost as he had planned it.

The sky was a little cloudy on Monday morning. Pa was in a real quandary. He didn't think it would rain until evening, and he wanted to get that haying done. But Ben Voth was pressing him for payment. Even though a good rain would be an answer to prayer, he wanted it to wait until he had his best prairie hay in the barn.

Matt had a bad moment when he thought his father might make him stay home and help with the haying. But Pa was persuaded that Matt would do the least work, and so he should be excused for this other errand. Matt resented the reason for his being chosen to make the trip, but his spirits rose as he put on clean overalls and got ready to go.

Pa had a last-minute instruction. "Ask for cash for the wheat. Mr. Voth wants cash for his payment. He is afraid to take a check. Put the cash in your shirt pocket under the bib of your overalls and button it shut."

John Paul went along, and Matt was glad for his company. John Paul was not the chatterbox that Vonnie was.

At seven, John Paul had Waldo's easygoing nature and Menno's willingness to please. His older sisters referred to him sometimes as their *Engeltji.* Their little angel had his own streak of determination, which everybody knew he had inherited from Pa. This trait was referred to as John Paul's *Buchsch,* or mulishness.

John Paul talked some and asked questions, but there were long stretches where Matt had his thoughts to himself.

Wellington was fifteen miles away, and it was a nice drive. After going three miles, he was out of the community that he knew. He crossed Bull Creek; then the dirt road narrowed and he was in a grove of locust trees, red hulls, and hickory. He was driving through bottom land, and after a time they came to the old bridge that crossed the Verdigris River, a wide, almost dry bed at this time of the summer. The new bridge was up river about a mile where there was less danger of flooding.

Matt wondered if the country would ever again have to worry about flooding.

On the west side of the river they passed prosperous-looking farms, such as those the Hadleys owned, with wide fields of pasture, strung off from ordinary farms with five strands of barbed wire on solid creosote posts. Sleek, grain-fed cattle roamed the rolling prairie, some Black Angus, some red Herefords, all beautiful to Matt's eyes. These pastures here seemed less parched than on his own farm, and Matt wondered why the rich had all the advantages.

And finally, just after eleven, there was Wellington. It was three times as big as Tansy, but it, too, told a story of Depression. There were homes with flaking paint and broken fences that in better times would have been repaired, and downtown there were closed-up stores. But business was still going on at the elevator, and Matt had to wait for a quarter of an hour before he could have his wheat weighed and unloaded.

After pocketing his money as Pa had told him to do, Matt drove the team into the shade and tied them to a fence post near the elevator. He fed them some oats, and he and John Paul ate the lunch of cold ham and bread that their mother had sent along.

Then Matt and John Paul walked up Main Street. It was a quiet Monday noon with little business activity. Matt paused outside the Wellington Bank and saw the banker through the big plate-glass window, looking very much like Mr. Schnell. Outside the bank three young men were sitting in a new model Ford, relaxed and laughing as Matt walked by. Matt wondered why they had the motor running. No doubt they were waiting for a pal in the bank.

He went on into the Mercantile Company next door to the bank to look at the refrigerators. He was lucky. They had one and he got the entry blank, although the owner who waited on him was clearly amused that he should want to enter the contest.

"Be sure to write on the entry blank that you got it here," he cautioned. "If you win, we get a prize, too, and I sure as shootin' don't want to miss out on it."

Matt left John Paul at the soda fountain of the Mercantile Company while he went over to the post office across the street. He filled out the entry blank with his twenty-five words and mailed it. He had a real sense of success as he dropped the envelope into the slot. He knew his twenty-five words were better than anybody else's because he, more than anybody else, wanted and needed that refrigerator and the five hundred dollars.

As he came out of the post office, he looked across the street at the bank and wondered what was different. He stopped on the sidewalk to think about it before crossing the street. Then he realized that the blind over the plate-glass window was pulled down. Funny that it should be down in the middle of the day. The bank at Tansy never closed during the noon hour. At that moment the blind rose with a slap that startled him. And through the front door burst two young men whom Matt had seen sitting in the Ford. One had a sack and one carried a gun.

They jumped on the running board of the car and it took off with a scream of tires. They headed out of town to the echo of their own laughter and gunshots.

At the sound of the shooting, storekeepers ran into the street and townspeople came from all directions. Within sixty seconds the dead street became alive with a milling mob.

Matt was one of the first to run into the bank to find the banker. He stood around as they untied the ropes and loosened the gag.

One man asked the banker, "Did you see them? Was it Floyd's gang?"

The banker sputtered, "Who else could it have been? One fellow called the other Charlie, didn't he? They surprised me so I couldn't even reach for my gun, and I keep one right here in the top drawer, too. I had been expecting this."

Matt remembered then that John Paul was waiting for him, and he ran back to the Mercantile Company. John

WELLINGTON · BANK · Co
1907
WELLINGTON
STEAM LAUNDR
OPEN
Jan Gleysteen

Paul was sitting there on the stool sipping his soda pop, all unaware of the commotion outside.

"Come on, we have to get home."

Matt helped him off the high stool, pausing for a moment to drink the last half inch from the bottle.

"There's been a bank robbery, and we had better get out of town and home before we get tangled up in it."

"Why?" asked John Paul. "You didn't have anything to do with it, did you?"

"Of course not, but I saw it happen. And I think I know who one of the gang is."

They walked down Main Street toward the elevator. The crowd was already beginning to disappear, and even though Matt loitered a little, nobody asked him any questions. He had rather hoped he could tell somebody that he had seen the men so he could describe them for the newspaper, but nobody asked him and he did not know whom to talk to. When it came right down to it, what would he say? He had seen three young guys laughing in front of the bank, but he couldn't remember what they had looked like, if they were light or dark, curly haired or not. He just had not looked at them that closely. Could he say that he thought the one called Charlie was his neighbor? Actually, he had never seen Charlie Boston close enough to know what he looked like.

They untied the team and started out of town. The horses stepped along smartly with the empty wagon.

"It's too bad," John Paul said.

"What's too bad?"

"That you didn't catch them and get the reward money. Vonnie says there is a reward for catching bank robbers."

"There is one for catching Pretty Boy Floyd. Three thousand dollars."

He certainly had missed his chance of getting the reward. They were probably on their way back to their hideout right now and they would stay there until they decided to pull another robbery, and nobody would find them because none of their relatives would tell where they were.

Matt wondered what he should have done to catch them. Should he have waited outside when they went in and then given the alarm and caught them as they came out, or warned the banker that they were parked out there, or made a dash from the post office and thrown himself in front of the car? Nothing seemed very practical. About all he could do now was to keep his ears and eyes open for Charlie Boston.

Another thought bothered him. Did he really have the kind of courage that it took to catch bank robbers? He remembered that at the moment when he had been looking at the bandit with the gun, his legs had felt like cooked spaghetti. He was exactly Windy John's idea of a Mennonite, no doubt.

6
Charlie Robs Two Banks

Matt was home from Wellington by the middle of the afternoon. He gave his mother the money and she told him to hurry out to the hay field without changing his clothes. He took Waldo's place on the rake and Waldo joined his father and Esther in gathering the hay and stacking it on the growing pile at the end of the field.

Waldo rushed him so much that Matt did not have time to tell him about the bank robbery. "Just let him be ignorant," Matt thought as he mounted the seat of the rake. "I'll make him sit up and take notice when I tell everybody when we have our afternoon lunch."

He was driving Jude and Jerry, and they made light work of turning the hay into a row so that the rack could drive along and pick it up easily.

One trouble Matt found with haying or cutting grain was that the little animals were driven from their homes. Mice were so little they hardly noticed you, and all they had to do was to keep away from the heels and wheels. But the young rabbits had to run. Still, they could take care of themselves. So could the skunks. When he saw the white stripe and the black plumed tail, Matt stopped the team until the skunks had made their leisurely getaway.

Soon after he started, Vonnie came out to the field with the lunch of jelly sandwiches and tea. They all welcomed the break, for the air was getting close and humid.

They sat in the shade of the new stack and talked about the clouds. "Do you think it will rain before we get done?" Waldo asked his father, the acknowledged weather prophet.

"Those clouds are too far away for rain until evening. They are moving too slow. Who is that stopping along the road?"

"That is Karl Berg's car," Esther said and then blushed. She put her hands up to tuck in the end of her braid.

Why should she get red in the face about Karl Berg? Matt wondered.

Karl came over to join them and Esther offered him a cup of tea. He could not wait to say the proper greetings before he exploded with his news.

"The bank at Fuller was robbed at noon today. You do your banking there, Pete?"

Fuller was just five miles north of Tansy, and many of the community went there to shop since it was a little bigger.

"You don't say!" Mr. Rempel exclaimed. "No, I do my banking at Tansy."

Waldo let out a whistle. "That's getting too close for comfort. Do they think it was the Floyd gang?"

"Who else?" Karl asked. "They even heard one fellow call the other one Charlie. That's Pretty Boy's name, you know."

"It wasn't the Floyd gang," Matt said knowingly.

Everyone turned to look at him in surprise.

"What do you know about it?" Waldo asked in a big-brother tone.

"I was in Wellington today at noon when the Floyd gang robbed that bank."

Surprise turned to astonishment, and Matt enjoyed the full attention of his audience.

"Matt!" Esther screamed. "Did they shoot at you?"

"No, they just shot up in the air, and I was about twenty feet away in front of the post office," he said calmly.

"That must have been some other gang, though," Karl Berg declared. "They said that one fellow distinctly called the other one Charlie in this Fuller holdup."

"The banker at Wellington said one fellow called the other one Charlie there, too, and I got a very good look at them before they went into the bank. I think one of them looked like the picture of Pretty Boy Floyd that hangs in the Tansy post office." Matt wondered just how far he was stretching the truth. But the more he thought about it, the more the bandit did look like that picture.

"Then they must have robbed the Wellington bank and then driven right over to Fuller and robbed that one," Waldo concluded.

"They said it was straight up twelve o'clock when they hit at Fuller," Karl said. "Somebody tried to shoot at them as they drove off but they got away slick as you please."

"It was straight up twelve when they came out of the bank at Wellington," Matt insisted. "I saw the clock in the post office."

Pa looked at the sky then and stood up. "Those clouds are moving faster than I thought. Come on, let's see if we can get this hay stacked and the tarp on before it rains. Was that lightning I saw way over there?"

Karl Berg said good-bye, thanking Esther very politely for the tea that she had had nothing to do with making. They all got back to their jobs in a hurry, and Matt urged Jude and Jerry on to new accomplishment.

Matt heard a bee buzz past his ear, and another and another. He realized then that he had driven over a nest in the hay. He slapped the reins on the mules' back, but at the same moment they got the message from the bees. They jumped straight up, which sent Matt and the seat of the rake down to the ground, and when the mules landed on their feet, they took off, prodded by the pursuing bees. Matt bounced back into the air, feeling as though he were on a teeter-totter that he couldn't control. He hung onto the reins because he had nothing else to hang on to, and although he pulled on them with all his thirteen-year-old muscles, the mules considered him and his rake as so much vanilla custard. They ran once around the field and then headed for the barnyard.

Matt could see his father and Waldo at the foot of the stack. He had a glimpse of Esther on top standing paralyzed as she watched him go around the stack once. Waldo and his father started running to head off the mules, but they couldn't catch up.

"Jump," they shouted, but Matt couldn't seem to let go of the reins.

They left the bees behind, but Jude and Jerry kept going, intoxicated with the joy of running. They entered the barnyard at a gallop and raced once around the barn.

Out of the corner of his eye, Matt saw his mother and Vonnie on the front porch, and he heard his mother scream, "Jump!"

The mules squeezed themselves and the rake between the hen house and the corncrib. They met a pile of fence posts that they jumped over as easily as if they were trained for the hunt. But only one wheel of the rake lifted up and over it. That was when Matt parted company with the rake. Pitched over in a horizontal position, he lost the reins and flew through the air in a gentle arc that sent him toward the horse tank by the windmill.

"I'm going to get my clean overalls wet," Matt, the washerwoman, thought as he saw the water rising to meet him.

The next moment he felt a sharp jag on his forehead and the water closing over him. He wondered why he felt so lifeless. "Because I'm dead," he decided simply, and that was his last thought.

He awoke to another time and another place. He was on a table in the doctor's office and his head ached. He put his hand up to find a good-sized bandage there. Then he realized that his clothes were wet and his shoes heavy. His mother was standing over him and she was almost as wet as he was.

Everybody tried to tell him in a babble how Mama had fished him out of the horse tank, his head covered with blood from the cut he got when he hit the edge of the tank. They had brought him to Tansy as fast as they could and were lucky to find the doctor in. Matt now had eight stitches in his forehead above his left eye.

"Boy, you belong in a rodeo," Waldo said, helping him to his feet. "Anybody who can drive a team of mules the way you do ought to go into the business."

"Thanks, Doc," Mr. Rempel said. "What's the charge?"

"That will be a dollar," Doc Shaeffer said. "Pay it when you have it."

They left, and Matt was glad to get away from the smell of the office. As they walked back to the car, Matt was surprised to see Windy John and Charlie Boston stop and hitch their wagon to the post in front of the doctor's house.

Matt tried to get a good look at Charlie, but Charlie had his straw hat pulled over his eyes so that Matt couldn't tell much about him. Charlie had one hand wrapped in a feed sack. Pa stopped to talk to Windy John while Mama and Waldo helped Matt into the car. When Pa joined them a few minutes later, he reported that the young man was John's nephew and that he had cut his hand with an ax while chopping kindling.

"That boy seems like a shy one," Pa observed. "Takes after his uncle that way."

They drove out of town, and as they went by the bank, Waldo said, "I wonder if Floyd's gang is going to try the Tansy Bank next. I hope Mr. Schnell doesn't keep a lot of cash on hand. They say the Prattville bank had to close its doors after it was robbed."

Mr. Rempel was optimistic. "They won't bother with a little place like Tansy," he assured Waldo.

Matt remembered something he had not thought about for a long time. "Windy John's nephew is named Charlie," he informed them.

But nobody gave this information much thought. "That

so?" Pa asked politely as he would humor any young boy who had just had his head gashed. Then he went on to explain to Waldo how bank robbers decide which bank to rob. Matt kept his thoughts to himself for the rest of the ride home. If nobody cared that Charlie "Pretty Boy" Floyd and Charlie Boston were the same person, they would sit up and take notice when he proved it to them.

As they drove by the hay field, Matt saw a figure waving to him from the top of the straw stack.

"Stop the car," he shouted to Waldo. "Did you leave Esther on top of the stack without a ladder?"

They had. Waldo drove right into the field. Esther was sputtering with anger. But her irritation soon turned to laughter as she described her plight.

"I sat up there for two hours thinking nobody loved me enough to miss me. I was afraid to slide down. I saw Matt get dunked in the stock tank and I saw you drive off for town. I didn't know whether he was dead or alive."

They returned to the barnyard to find the mules standing patiently waiting for someone to untangle them from the fence where they had caught the rake. There was no damage to themselves, the fence, or the rake.

Then Pa remembered to look at the sky to see how the storm was building up, and they were surprised to find that all signs of it had disappeared with the daylight. The air was still muggy and hot, however.

Matt was installed on the couch in the kitchen and was pampered by the rest of the family.

John Paul declared that he looked peaked. "I could give you a blood confusion," he offered.

"No thank you," Matt said firmly. "I've had enough

confusion for today. Just sit there and keep me company."

Vonnie joined them. "I can entertain you. I'll tell you a joke. Did you hear about the fellow who said that the liniment made his arm smart, and the other fellow said, 'Then why don't you rub some on your head?' See, if he rubbed it on his head, it might make his head—"

"No more jokes," Matt interrupted.

Mama tucked Matt into bed and then brought him a cup of water from the bucket by the sink. "The doctor says for you to drink lots of water to make up for your loss of blood," she urged.

The water was tepid and not refreshing, but he drank it to please her. He handed back the empty cup and said, "Ma, how would you like to have a refrigerator that makes ice?"

His mother smiled and smoothed the sheet. "That's for heaven, Matthew."

After his mother left him, Matt had time finally to think more about Charlie. Charlie had been hurt. Matt did not believe that story about his cutting himself with an ax. Charlie had been nicked by a bullet as he and his gang had fled out of town after robbing the Fuller bank. He must have been in Fuller. Matt had not recognized him as one of the gang in Wellington. Everything seemed to be making sense, Matt was convinced. Charlie Boston was an alias for Charlie Floyd. The only fact Matt was not sure about was whether Windy John knew of Charlie's bank-robbing activities.

"There ought to be some way to catch a bank robber who lives only a mile across the field," Matt thought, but he fell asleep before he could work out all the details.

7
The Storm

By late August the drought was a very serious problem.

"It seems that we have less rain every year," Mr. Rempel said one morning, scanning the sky for rain clouds.

Matt stood beside him on the porch, looking off into the northwest, the direction from which rain would come—if it came. There had not been a good soaking rain all summer. Crooked Creek was completely dry for the first time in history, with large smooth slabs of fried mud crisscrossed by wide cracks.

For a real soaking, cooling-off, cleaning-off swim, the Rempel men had to go to the quarry on the back of the Ben Voth farm. There the bank dropped sharply to a bottomless pit that had once been a gravel quarry.

The quarry was fed by an artesian well that bubbled continuously. When someone threw a match at the source of the well, the water seemed to ignite and burn. The explanation was, of course, that there was natural gas escaping with the water and the gas did the burning. It made a pleasant light to swim by at night.

But the days were dust-filled. The dust blew from the

stubble fields and the roads. If it came from across the road, it made a gray film over Mama's library table. If it came from the east, it was red, varying from mahogany to orange. Sometimes you could look at a cloud of dust on the horizon and see different shades and know from what parts of Oklahoma, Texas, or Kansas the cloud had picked up its load.

The hay meadows were dry and brown. The cattle had eaten everything they could find in the barren pastures and had been moved to a meadow on the Plank place because there was a spring there that had never failed. Once a day Matt and Waldo went over to start the windmill so that the tank could be filled; or, if there was no wind, to pump water by hand for the fifty head of cattle. They had to carry water for family use from the Plank place, too. The cistern was dry.

The cornfields were a sorry sight. The ears had not matured, and the stalks stood in the fields, dusty and dry. Mr. Rempel ordered the boys to feed the stalks to the cows for forage.

And this was only August. "How will we get the cattle through the winter?" they asked of nobody in particular, for nobody had an answer.

Money was as scarce as rain. Mama barely got enough eggs and cream to buy the staple groceries of flour and sugar, and Pa had nothing to sell from the farm. He counted heavily on the money that the older children brought home from their jobs.

Les had a steady job and felt lucky to be earning forty dollars a month during the summer and thirty dollars during the winter months. Menno said he wished he could find work like that. His job with Ben Voth would be over as soon as the fall plowing was finished. He needed the work and he thought he needed the money. His greatest dream was to have a car of his own, and if he could get one hundred dollars ahead, he knew just what he would buy. Bill Jantz was leaving for California and wanted to sell his new car to whoever would take over the monthly installments.

"You couldn't pay for a car with the little Pa gives you to spend," Matt reminded him.

"I know. But maybe times will be better and Pa won't need my wages. Anyway, I like to think about it," Menno said. "With that car I could have me a good time," he confided to Matt as they were washing up for supper. "I would take out a blonde from Tansy on Monday and a brunette from Wellington on Tuesday."

At the supper table when Menno asked if he could use the Model T that evening, Pa grumbled, "Why can't you boys be satisfied with courting the way we did it? Every two weeks I hitched up the buggy and went to see your Ma."

"Ach, Pa. Don't be old-fashioned," Menno answered. "This is a modern age."

"Well, you won't live modern with my money. If you use my car, you can buy the gas."

One Sunday night in late August the church had a farewell party for Bill Jantz. Bill had sold his car to Karl Berg, and he was all packed into one suitcase ready to hitchhike his way to California. He had a ride with a traveling salesman as far as Albuquerque. The job in his cousin's creamery would be ready for him in two weeks.

Lightning was playing in the northwest as the Rempels drove home from the party, and they went to bed hoping for a real rain this time, but the morning brought bright sun and a light wind. It had rained in some place, but not in the Tansy area.

On Monday noon the mail carrier left a card saying that there was a package addressed to Matt at the Tansy post office, too large to be delivered. Would he please pick it up? Matt knew immediately what it was. His refrigerator! But why had they sent it parcel post? He had expected it by freight at the depot in Tansy. How long would he have to wait to get to Tansy to pick it up?

Pa gave instructions at the dinner table for work to be done that afternoon while he and Mama went to a funeral in Tansy. "Cut a load of fodder for the cattle and take it over to the Plank place. Make sure the cattle have plenty of water."

Matt gave his father the card and asked him to pick up the package. Although Pa was curious about it, Matt would not explain.

In the late afternoon Waldo and Matt hitched the mules to the hayrack and went to the field for a load of fodder. Then they drove the two miles to the Plank place to feed the cattle. John Paul drove Beauty and the pony cart with the milk can, for they would have to milk the cows and bring back the milk. John Paul's dog Spud trotted along behind.

When they reached the Plank place, they noticed thunderheads moving in from the northwest.

Waldo commented, "It looks like another teaser. I wonder why there isn't any lightning."

All three of the boys took a milk stool from the pony cart and started milking the ten cows in the herd. By the time they were through milking, the clouds had moved overhead and the wind was rising, bringing with it little whirlwinds of dust. They loaded the milk can in the back of the pony cart.

Waldo called to John Paul, "You hurry now, John Paul, and get home before this storm hits. Matt and I will come home as soon as we get the cattle fed and watered."

John Paul obeyed, and the pony added dust to dust as he ran toward home pulling the little cart.

Matt hurried to release the brake of the windmill, and there was soon a two-inch stream of water flowing into the tank. Waldo was at the end of the field ready to throw the corn fodder off the rack.

Then the storm struck. The wind was so strong that Matt stopped the windmill; and the sky was so black that he could not see Waldo at the end of the field. Matt was puzzled for a minute about the rain, but then he realized that it was not raining but blowing a blizzard of dust. He ran to the gatepost, which was an upright railroad tie, and sat on the sheltered side, holding his hands over his face to protect his eyes and nose from the dust. There was a flash in the darkness and a crackling of thunder. Then mercifully the rain came in long wind-driven slashes.

Matt felt something nuzzling his hands and face, and for a terrified moment thought it was a coyote, but he opened his eyes to find Spud begging for a place on his lap. Quivering and shaking, the wet dog curled up in his arms, cowering from the thunder. They sat there, shivering together, hail bouncing like marbles around them.

After about ten minutes the rain slackened a little, but the wind kept roaring in from the west. Suddenly, the hail was over.

Waldo had not come back. Matt wondered what to do. Finally, dumping the startled Spud from his lap, he got up and looked for Waldo and the rack. The sky was lighter now, and he could see it at the end of the field. He started walking toward it, keeping close to the fence so that he wouldn't be blown away. He found the mules against the fence with their backs turned to the wind. Waldo was hanging on to the side of the rack to keep it from blowing over and Matt joined him, adding his hundred pounds of weight.

Finally Waldo said, "I believe it's about blowed out. Let's see if we can get these mules untangled."

The wind had done their unloading for them by flinging the fodder into the feed lot, and the cloudburst had finished filling the stock tank.

"I wonder if John Paul got home before it hit," Matt said as they jogged home through the quiet rain.

When they passed Crooked Creek School, they saw Beauty and the pony cart standing in the open barn.

Waldo said, "Well, I guess John Paul is waiting out the rain in the school barn. Say, look at that barn. The roof has blown off! Where's John Paul?"

With mounting dread, the boys looked for their brother, but he was nowhere around the school grounds.

"The little guy must have blown into the next county," Waldo exclaimed. "Come on, let's get home and tell the folks. We should get the neighbors out looking for him."

Matt untied the pony and the cart and followed Waldo

home. He had thoughts of his brother lying crushed and unwhimpering in some far-off field.

They put the mules into the barn without unharnessing them and rushed to the house. They found Vonnie in the front room trying to clean up the flood that had come in by a broken west window.

John Paul was sitting in the middle of his parents' bed trying to wrap an entire flour sack around his finger.

"Where have you been?" Vonnie demanded. "The wind blew out the window and the rain soaked the bed."

"It looks as though you have been busy," Matt observed, looking around the room at the furniture that had been moved out of the way of the rain.

"Lightning hit the chimney and the bricks fell into the front room and the soot got all over the organ, and I had to shoo the chickens into the coops and drag Donald into the barn, and John Paul came home with his hand bleeding," she elaborated. "Have I been busy?" And then her bustling tone changed, and Vonnie was brimming over with self-pity. "I was all by myself and I didn't know what to do. Where were you?" She burst into tears.

John Paul looked after her in wonder. "She wasn't crying when I came home. Look, I cut my finger."

Matt and Waldo watched him unroll the mile of bandage so they could examine his cut. "We looked all over for you. What happened?" Waldo asked.

"When I saw those black clouds and the wind started to blow, I hitched up in the barn to wait a while, but the wind blew the roof off so I tried to get into the schoolhouse, but it was locked. Then I found a broken window, so I crawled in." John Paul told his story calmly.

"What did you do in there? Weren't you scared?" Matt asked.

"Yes, I was scared. I prayed the whole time. I prayed and prayed for hours. Well, I did fall asleep, but I didn't sleep very long because a' nold mouse ran over my foot and it tickled, so I crawled out of the window and came home."

"Did you walk home?"

"No, I ran. Say, I forgot about Beauty. I'd better go get poor old Beaut."

Before anyone could explain to him, Mr. and Mrs. Rempel came in the door.

"How do you like this rain?" Pa shouted cheerfully. "It won't save the crops, but it is wet. We can plow."

And Mama said, "We can plant a little garden."

Vonnie came, dry-eyed now, to tell her story, and the boys interrupted each other to tell theirs.

"Where were you when the storm hit?" Matt asked his parents.

"We had left the graveyard and were driving toward home," Pa answered. "I had snapped on the side curtains in case it might rain, and I was glad I had when that dust started to blow. Then all of a sudden a cornstalk blew right through the top of the car and lay on the back seat. I was so surprised I almost went off the road."

"I made him stop off at Amish Yoders' until the wind was over," Mama said.

"They made us very welcome," Pa continued. "They fixed coffee and wanted us to stay for supper. They were getting ready for church at their place next Sunday. Such a housecleaning!"

"Which Yoders would they be?" Waldo asked.

"Nancy John Yoders," Pa replied. At Matt's incredulous look, he added, "His mother's name was Nancy so they called him Nancy John to keep him straight with all the other John Yoders."

"Very plain people, but very nice. No curtains at the windows, but lots of geraniums," Mama commented. "And such pretty china in the sideboard."

"Mama, did I ever mention how these Amish are different from those I knew in Canada? Here they wear two suspenders and those I knew wore only one." Pa took an interest in the customs of different churches.

"Well, they were very nice to us," Mama said, "even if we do wear buttons instead of hooks and eyes."

"Say," Pa snapped his fingers. "I forgot to bring in your parcel."

Matt had forgotten about his refrigerator, too, in the excitement of the storm. He ran out to the car wondering how you could call even a small refrigerator a parcel. When he lifted the box, he knew that this was not the answer to his prayers. He wondered if it was anything. The box was about as heavy as a package of marshmallows.

With growing disappointment, he took the box into the kitchen and pried it open. The family gathered around, wondering and questioning, as Matt got the top off and began pulling out the excelsior packing.

"Come on, chatterbox, tell us what you have there," Waldo chided impatiently.

Finally Matt spoke. "I entered a contest."

"Oh, you won a prize," Vonnie squealed.

Matt dived into the box and pulled out a tall table

lamp. The bottom part was a bright yellow and red vase with handles on each side. The shade was of parchment with large red roses. It was a very colorful lamp.

Mama said, "It is beautiful. And to think you won it as a prize."

Vonnie's eyes popped when she saw it. "I have never seen anything so pretty," she breathed.

Even Pa was impressed. "What kind of a contest?"

Matt, feeling better about the situation, answered, "I wrote twenty-five words about why I wanted a refrigerator, and I guess this was one of the prizes."

Waldo picked up the lamp and carried it into the front room. He placed it reverently in the middle of the library table.

"There is just one thing about it. It's an electric light. Too bad we don't have electricity."

"That doesn't matter," Mama said. "It is so pretty. Just hide the cord behind the table."

For the first time, Matt was struck by the fact that if he had won an electric refrigerator, they couldn't have used it. How could he have been so stupid? Under the circumstances the lamp was really a better prize. The summer would soon be over, the heat would surely now be broken by the rain, and a refrigerator was not so important. The five hundred dollars had never been more than a dream anyway. He hadn't counted on it the way he had counted on the refrigerator or the way he still counted on that oil well.

All during supper Matt could feel his father's eyes on him. Pa said little during the whole meal, and after everyone had left the table and only he and Ma were sitting over their coffee, he called Matt back to the table. But it was Mama he talked to. "Mama, we have a clever boy, yah? He can write words that win a contest."

Was his father making fun of him?

"Mama, maybe we don't ask 'what good is it,' schooling, I mean. Maybe we just say you and I didn't need more than third grade; but our children, they need more and better than we did."

He got up then and went to light the lantern and join the boys in finishing the chores.

What did he mean by that last speech? It sounded as though he was saying that he had changed his mind about a boy's not needing more schooling. Matt stood at the window watching the dark and quiet rain. For the first time in days he allowed himself a hint of hope that Pa might change his mind.

The saving rain continued during the night, but Matt awoke to a world covered with the shine of water and sun. He imagined that the trees looked greener.

When he went to milk the cows, there was the almost forgotten joy of sinking his toes into the mud of the feed lot. He milked Kicker and Hardtail, and the milk splashed into the bucket to the rhythm of the music in his mind.

When he came to Rosie, the music he had in his head burst forth. Rosie was an easy milker, but she had to be sung to. So in his changing voice Matt treated Rosie to the lilting words of "Redwing." The ballad told the story of a mournful Indian maiden whose brave had been killed. Rosie was so pleased that her milk came down as easily as if she had turned on a faucet.

When he got back to the house, Matt called John Paul

out to watch a cardinal in the pecan tree by the back porch. John Paul stood looking up into the leaves. On sudden impulse, Matt caught a branch and shook it hard, and the rain showered John Paul so that he ducked back onto the porch, wet as a muskrat. The little boy laughed.

"If Menno had done that to me, I would have been mad," Matt thought. "Life would be a lot easier if I didn't take things so hard."

He didn't have time to dwell on the nature of Matthew, however. Karl Berg drove in to report that Windy John's farm had been leveled by the wind. Only the house had been left standing. The neighbors were meeting there today to help clean up. Pa, Waldo, and Matt dropped their work and went over to help with the cleanup and to build a new barn.

The lumber dealer in Tansy had agreed to deliver all the material they needed. With the prospect of the oil well that would be coming in shortly, the lumber company was glad enough to take a mortgage on John's farm. The neighbors brought their own saws and hammers and crowbars. They took their orders from carpenter John Yoder, an Amishman well known for his good work.

Every denomination of Mennonites turned out for the barn raising. Although most of them could not attend each other's churches, except for funerals, they all felt that they could help a neighbor who was in trouble.

The younger men, including Matt and Cornie, went to working picking up and stacking boards from the buildings that had blown down. Matt was hoping for the opportunity to satisfy his curiosity about Windy John's nephew. But as he worked around with the other boys, he could see no sign of Charlie Boston. Either he was gone or in hiding.

Matt's father suggested that he round up the chickens, so Matt went to ask Windy John what he should do about them. He found his neighbor amidst a pile of debris by the back porch.

"One thing about a wooden leg," Windy John said wryly, "you don't know when you step on a nail."

"You don't have to worry about lockjaw if you do, either," Matt replied.

"No, I just worry about how I'm going to pay all these people for all this work."

"You can't pay them. They aren't doing this for pay," Matt assured him.

"I've always given a day's work for a day's work to my neighbors. That's the only way to get along with people."

Waldo approached from the granary. "What shall we do with that wheat?" he asked, pointing back to a pile that lay exposed after the splintered boards of the granary had been removed.

"Put it in the west room of the house," Windy John answered. "I will move my bed into the kitchen." Waldo nodded and strode off.

Matt asked, "And what about the chickens after we have them rounded up?"

"Put them in the east room. Charlie can move his cot into the kitchen, too."

When Windy John noticed Matt's surprised expression, he said hastily, "It's only for a few days until I have a place in the barn. I don't mind chickens."

Karl Berg came up to ask what to do with the hogs.

Matt waited for Windy John to say, "Put them in the kitchen," but he looked at Matt, quirked an eyebrow, and said, "Keep them in the wagon until we get a pen built."

When Karl trotted off to take care of the hogs, Windy John turned to Matt. "Matt, I want you to meet my nephew. I think it would do him good to know your family." He called into the house, "Charlie, come here."

A slight, shy figure appeared in the doorway.

"Charlie, meet my neighbor, Matt Rempel. Matt, this is Charlie."

The boys said "hello" and shook hands, and then Charlie backed into the house without trying to make conversation. Matt was so busy looking at Charlie that he forgot his manners. In that half-minute of observation, he decided that Charlie Boston looked to be about twenty-one, probably about Bill Jantz's age. He tried to compare his looks with those of Pretty Boy Floyd, as he remembered him from pictures in the papers. Charlie was fair and Pretty Boy was dark, but that didn't prove anything. Matt had read that criminals had been known to bleach their hair when they wanted a disguise, so Charlie's hair could have been any color.

"That Charlie is a good boy," Windy John was saying. "Don't let nobody tell you different. And I'll tell you something I don't want anybody else to know. He ain't my nephew exactly."

Matt was surprised by this piece of news, but then he realized that he should not have been. There had always seemed to be something unusual about the relationship.

"He came to me needin' a job. He had been in the reformatory over to Kansas City and he was on probation.

He couldn't get a job and he needed a chance to prove he could make it as an honest man. He is determined not to get into no trouble, and I want to help him."

Matt regarded Windy John with increasing respect. "That's real good of you."

Windy John said, "Now you don't need to tell nobody about this. It will be easier if nobody knows. But since you are a friend of mine, I didn't want to be lyin' about anything to you. I do sort of think of him as my nephew now."

The old man turned to answer the questions of the barn raisers, and Matt started hunting the homeless chickens. Charlie did seem like a nice, quiet fellow. But those quiet ones were the troublemakers. Matt wondered what he had done to have deserved the reformatory sentence.

Matt was sure by this time that Windy John did not know that Charlie was mixed up with a gang of bank robbers. Matt felt sorry for Windy John, but he didn't let his sympathy overwhelm him. Not that Matt *wanted* Charlie to be a criminal. But if he was a criminal, he wanted him to be Pretty Boy Floyd. There was that reward money to think about. Sooner or later someone was bound to capture Pretty Boy and win the three thousand dollars. It could be Matthew Rempel, Boy Sheriff.

It was now August. Could he win the reward before school started in September? That might take a miracle.

8
Windy John's Oil Well Comes In

Matt had to watch Vonnie and John Paul start back to school in September. No miracle had happened to make it possible for him to go to high school.

"What would you study if you did go to school?" John Paul asked as Matt helped him and Vonnie harness Beauty and hitch her to the pony cart. "Haven't you had all the courses there are?"

"I would take geometry, literature, typing, Latin—"

"Latin is a dead language," Vonnie said. "My teacher said so."

"Do you plan to be an undertaker, Matt?" John Paul asked.

"No, I am going to take physiology and be a fizzle, or biology and be a biolinist."

"You could take weaving and be a weevil," Vonnie suggested, entering into the spirit of things.

Vonnie liked school, but she hated walking the two miles back and forth.

Matt scolded her for complaining. "You should be humbly grateful that you can go to school."

"I feel more like being grumbly hateful," she declared impiously.

That first week in September, Matt's spirits were lower than the Verdigris River. There was nothing to look forward to but the dull routine of plowing. The Rempel farm was the most uninteresting, tedious, cheerless spot in the world. God, looking down from his heaven, must have seen a vast patchwork of wheat fields being plowed, and Matt Rempel was an ant plodding up and down the half-mile furrows, pushing two mules that skittered like cockroaches or poked along like snails.

But there was a morning that was so fresh and shining that the mules, Jerry and Jude, stepped along lively as ladybugs, and Matt felt more like a man than an ant. He had contrived a method of churning by fastening the bucket of cream under the seat of his plow so that it sloshed along, making butter without any effort on his part. Matt was elated that he had thought of an invention that Waldo had approved of. Even his father had commented on his cleverness.

The Rempel wheat field bordered Windy John Boston's hay meadow, and Matt had a good view of the oil derrick as he drove the team toward the south end of the field. Work had been going on there all summer, and Matt had visited the well now and then to see what was happening. Usually there was not much to see. The drill kept working; the men watched it, took care of the machinery, changed the bit when it became dull.

But this morning there seemed to be some excitement around the well. Matt could see more men and cars coming and going. He thought about slipping over to see what was happening, but his father had impressed on him only that morning that they needed to keep working steadily to get the plowing done.

Surprisingly, Jerry and Jude became his benefactors. When the mules reached the south end of the field, they stopped at the end of the row and would not budge. There were times when Jude took a spell to be very contrary, and Matt reckoned that this was one of those mornings. Without even trying to get him over his mulishness, Matt tied the animals to the fence and ran to the oil derrick.

He was surprised to find Waldo already there, right in the middle of things, learning all he could about oil drilling. But most surprising was the presence of Charlie Boston looking over Waldo's shoulder. Evidently his interest in the well had helped him to overcome enough of his shyness to mingle with the men.

The oil crew was paying close attention to the cuttings that were being flushed up to the surface. The seismologist was there, a man Matt recognized from previous visits.

Windy John was standing off to the side, and Matt joined him. "Are you looking for a gusher today?" Matt asked.

Windy John shook his head. "There won't be no gusher here. A gusher is a well out of control, and these fellows are too smart to let anything like that happen. See that young chap looking through that mud? He can tell by smelling it and tasting it just how close he is to oil. They'll be ready for it when it comes."

The two sat down on a pile of pipe and Windy John asked, "Ever hear of Spindletop?"

Matt nodded. "Down in Texas."

Scammel
OKLAHOMA 1931
BEG-10-2

"About thirty years ago. That was a gusher, all right. There was an explosion of mud and water and the Hamill boys climbed down from the derrick and ran. They saw the drill pipe come shootin' up from the earth, and then all that mile of pipe broke up into sections and came raining down. Wrecked the derrick and the crown block. They were gettin' ready to clean up the mess, and here comes another explosion. More mud and rock, and then gas and then oil. That well was out of control for ten days."

Matt asked, "What happened to all that oil?"

"Captain Lucas, the owner, hired forty teams of four horses each and built reservoirs. He hired an army of fifty men to stand watch day and night, but then somebody lit a cigar. You never saw such billows of smoke and flame. Everybody pitched in and they put it out, but they had other fires."

"I hope they don't let anything like that happen here," Matt said.

"There was a gusher at Oklahoma City just three years ago. Stout Fella came in and splashed sixty thousand barrels of oil over houses and office buildings, and even the state Capitol. A real mess."

"It sure tests my patience to wait for it. Ain't you anxious, Mr. Boston?"

"Oh, I'll take it when it comes."

The call came to change the drill bit, and the two sat there silently watching as the roughnecks hauled length after length of pipe from the hole, stacking the ninety-foot sections in the rack in the derrick until finally they would bring up the bit.

Windy John said, "What makes you so itchy about this

well? Do you think maybe the Company will drill on your Pa's place?"

Matt did not know how much to tell of his dream of an oil well. "They might," he said cautiously, but in a moment he found himself carried away in telling Windy John of his hopes that an oil well might mean he could go on to high school and of his half-hope that his father would let him go.

The old man looked at him skeptically. "Why should a sensible boy like you want to go to school? I had school to third grade, and I get along. You aimin' to be a college professor or something like that?"

Matt shook his head. "No. I like to study. Mr. Boston, do you think it is wrong to want to go to high school? If God didn't plan for us to learn things, why did he put things on earth to learn about?"

Windy John studied a while, digging at the hard ground with the tip of his leg. "No, I don't think it is wrong to want to learn. Of course, you can learn things without goin' to school."

Windy John shifted his position on the pile of pipe and abruptly changed the subject. "Matt, tell me something. Why did these neighbors of mine come over to help me out last month?"

"Because they are your neighbors, that's all. They wanted to help you."

"I never helped any of them. It's always a day's work for a day's work when we do something for each other."

"Well, Mr. Boston, I don't know if I can tell you in the right words, but we believe that we should help share the troubles of our neighbors when we can."

Windy John gave him a sharp look. "Does this have anything to do with your church's peace talk?"

"Yes, I guess so. We believe that we should not go to war and take the life of another person; but we believe, too, that we should help people live."

Windy John shook his head. "I don't remember anything in the Bible about helpin' a man build his barn."

Matt smiled. "We are supposed to feed the hungry, clothe the naked, visit the sick, and rebuild the barn that is blown down. Matthew 25. That was the Sunday school lesson two weeks ago."

Windy John smiled too and ran his fingers through his rumpled hair. "Now, I don't mean I don't appreciate the help your churches gave me. But I don't think you can make up in good works for your lack of courage when it comes to fightin'."

"In the last war, my Uncle Chris in Kansas went to jail rather than join the army. He was chained in a prison in California. I think he was brave for standing up for something he believed in."

"I ain't sayin' there's only one kind of bravery," Windy John admitted. "But I think you have to be willin' to give your life for what you believe in. Surely you believe in your country."

Matt felt that he was getting beyond his depth, but he wanted desperately to make Windy John see his point of view. "We do believe in giving our own lives for what we believe in, but we don't believe in killing other people. It is hard for me to explain it. Shall I have the preacher tell you about it?"

"No, no," Windy John said hastily. "You said it all

right." He looked around for a change of subject. "Did you notice Charlie over there? I'm hopin' that he is comin' out of his little gopher hole. I always wondered if he was so shy before he got into that trouble with the law. He seems like a friendly kid, but he has always been jumpy as a guinea hen. I think he has been afraid somebody would find out about the reformatory and make a fuss about it."

"Maybe he is like Waldo. He can't stay away from machinery," Matt said.

"I doubt if he saw much machinery in those Kansas City streets where he grew up." Windy John looked toward the Rempel wheat field. "Say, looks to me like your mules are gettin' restless. I don't think this wildcat is goin' to tear in today, anyhow. They won't even get that bit changed for another two hours."

Matt went back to his plow. Jude and Jerry were ready to go again, and he urged them to a steady pull to try to make up for the time he had played hooky. Even so, noon came before he had done his half-day's work, and he took his churned butter and went in to dinner.

That evening after supper, Matt went to look under the bed for the box of books that Pa had brought home from the sale. He was interested in one title that he remembered, *A Dictionary of Thoughts.* This was a dusty volume, old and yellowed but apparently not much read. It was a book of quotations listed by subjects, starting with Ability and ending with Zeal.

Matt was interested in Courage. Sure enough, there was a section on courage and there were several quotations that spoke to his feelings.

"No man can answer for his courage who has never

been in danger." Had there ever been a time when his courage had been really tested? He knew that he often felt scared that something might happen, such as the time of the bank robbery. What had he been afraid of then? Of getting hurt, he supposed. But he had not had much of an opportunity to show courage then because everything had happened so fast.

"Moral courage is a virtue of higher cast and nobler origin than physical." Now there you had the case of Uncle Chris. He had had the moral courage to accept imprisonment and torture rather than to do what was against his conscience.

Did he, Matthew, nephew of Chris, have moral courage? Again, he didn't know. He had never been tested.

He went on in the book for the fun of finding quotations. Then he started looking at the names of the men who had said these things. Ruskin, Rochefoucauld, Dryden, Plato, Confucius, Shakespeare. Who were they? The only one he had ever heard of was Shakespeare. What kind of man was George Eliot? There was no book in the Rempel house that could answer his questions.

Matt looked for quotations on oil wells, but the closest he could come to the subject was wealth, which was about the same idea.

Matt put the book away for another time. Quotations were very filling reading, and it didn't take a lot of them to satisfy his appetite.

Windy John's well did come in the next day, but Matt did not see it at the moment when the oil started to flow. Matt, Waldo, and their father went over that afternoon to congratulate Windy John on his good fortune.

"It isn't much of a flow," Windy John commented. "The Oil Company is real disappointed in it."

Mr. Fenwig sauntered up. "I feel sure that around here someplace is a good oil pool. It is hard to hit these sandstone shoestrings in this country, but Mr. Capley believes they are here. This one is just a teaser, not much commercial value to it."

Windy John and the Company made an agreement by which John would take care of the well himself and market the oil. "You can milk it just like a cow," Mr. Fenwig said. "You'll get five, ten barrels a day. That's not much petroleum jelly as far as the Company is concerned, but if the price stays at a dollar a barrel, it will give you a little income."

The crew removed the derrick and installed a "Christmas tree" contraption of valves to control the flow of the oil. They told Windy John that he could put a pump on it when the natural pressure slowed down. Then the Company pulled out.

"I would have liked to have had a gusher for one reason," Windy John confessed as he and Matt watched Mr. Fenwig drive off. "If I had a good oil well, I would buy another eighty for Charlie. He seems to be takin' hold of farmin'. But I guess he will have to make his own way."

Matt was more disappointed in the well than Windy John was. If the well had produced a spectacular flow, the Company might have wanted to come over to the Rempel land and try one there. It was Company policy to drill an equal distance from the boundary line of two properties so that one owner could not accuse the other of draining the oil from his land.

Matt went back to the routine task of farming, mostly plowing, again. He helped feed the cattle and milk the cows; he went to church and spent time with Cornie. When his mother needed him, he stayed around the house to wash and iron. He tried as much as possible to put the well out of his mind, for it seemed to be a lost cause.

One Friday evening after milking, Mr. Rempel had a visitor. Mr. Fenwig was back. The Company had decided to buy up leases around the country in an effort to hit the oil pool that they knew was there. They would like to take a lease on the Rempel eighty. Mr. Fenwig was ready to pay cash.

The whole family sat out on the porch to listen to his glowing talk. "We would like to pay you one dollar an acre for the privilege of drilling for oil on your land. Then if we strike oil, you will get a royalty of eight percent of what we pump out. If we produce only one hundred barrels a day, that would be two hundred forty dollars a month for you. Think of what you could do with that money."

Matt thought: There would be money for me to go to high school. And then, he thought quickly, guiltily, the family could get some things. A new car, a load of hogs, and a new room to the house.

Mama asked Mr. Fenwig if he would like to stay for supper, and he surprised them all by accepting without any hemming or hawing. They had quite an ordinary meal, Matt thought; there were the same old fried potatoes, ham, cream gravy, tomatoes, rye bread, and canned peaches. Mr. Fenwig could not get over complimenting Mama on the fine meal.

"Mrs. Rempel, you should be cooking for one of the big hotels in Tulsa. Why, this meal would be worth a dollar anywhere. The rye bread alone would be worth the price of the meal."

Matt wondered what Mr. Fenwig would say if Mama fed him some of the German dishes, *Borscht* or *Wareneki* or *Moos.* Then he would really sit up and beg.

That very evening Mr. Fenwig wrote out a check for eighty dollars. Handing it to Pa with great ceremony, he said, "I hope yours is the one. Good luck to you."

He shook hands all around the family and left.

"That's more money than I have seen for a long time," Pa said, closing the door after him.

"What will you do with it?" Vonnie asked. "I would like a dinner pail. All the other kids carry nice dinner pails but I have this old molasses bucket."

"I'll get a new suit and a pair of shoes," Menno said. He was at home now that his job was over. "My old suit is too short for me. The soles on my shoes are so thin that when I scratch a match on them, I tear my socks."

Waldo wanted a new canvas top for the car.

"I'll take a sack of sugar," Mama said.

But John Paul had the strangest request. "I want a pole."

"What kind of pole? What do you want a pole for?" demanded Menno.

"I want a pole-vaulting pole. I'm going to learn to pole-vault."

Nobody was surprised. "Go find yourself a good stout stick," Pa suggested. "No, this money is going into the bank."

"Why put it in the bank?" Waldo asked. "We can spend it on things we need tomorrow."

"I want to look around for some hogs. The paper says that in hogs there is hope for prosperity. Hogs and cattle will pull the country out of the Depression."

Pa had the last word. Matt looked at his mother with her troubled face, but she didn't say anything. He knew that she didn't trust banks.

Pa, as if in answer to the unspoken thought, said, "I saw Mr. Schnell the other day and he said things are getting better and his bank is sounder than it ever was."

"Come, it is dark," Mama said, not arguing. "You should all be in bed."

His brothers and sister left the kitchen to prepare for bed, but Matt lingered. He wanted to discuss a subject with his father.

"I just can't believe it," he began carefully. "Wouldn't an oil well solve all our problems?"

Mama sat with her hands folded quietly in her lap. "I won't think about it. We have worked hard all our lives, and I feel that the Lord intends for us to work the rest of the time. Oil money isn't for people like us."

"Now, Mama," Pa protested, "we don't know what the Lord intends. Maybe he wants to give us a little grace. I know that an oil well won't help our children to grow up to be better people; but if it comes, we will use it."

"Pa," Matt spoke hesitantly, "Pa, if we had oil money, could I go back to school? I mean, do you think I could go to high school?"

Pa's face lost its fun. "We've talked about this before. You know there is more to this than the money. How can we farm three hundred acres unless we have men, and you will soon be able to work like a man."

Matt was encouraged by this last idea. He had wondered if his family would ever consider him a man.

Mama said gently, "Do you need schooling to be a farmer?"

"Yes, Mama. I would like to have schooling before I am anything. I would like to read all the books and work all the problems and do all the experiments. I don't know if I will be a farmer. I don't know what I will be."

Mr. Rempel spoke up sharply. "And I suppose you would like to play all the basketball games, go to all the parties, and court all the English girls."

Matt watched as his mother took careful stitches in an overall patch. "Not if you say not to."

His father's voice softened. "We Mennonites are a people of one Book. If you want to read, there is the Bible. Everything has been said there. We are afraid you won't be interested in the church after you get educated. You would marry outside and move away."

Marry! The idea of marriage was too far distant to even be considered.

Mama leaned over and patted his hand. "Matt is a good boy, Papa."

"But I can't afford to hire a man while he goes to high school," Pa said.

Matt looked up with sudden hope. "Then if we strike oil, I might be able to go to high school?"

Pa shook his head and stood up, taking Ma's patchwork out of her hands. "What do we do with such a boy who won't take no for an answer? Send him to bed!"

9
Money Comes—and Goes

Pa did go to town the next afternoon to bank his lease money, taking Menno and Waldo along with him. Menno wanted to inquire around about work for the winter and Waldo wanted to go to the junkyard for material for fixing the top of the car where the cornstalk had plunged through. They would soon need the protection from the cold and wind, and from the rain in case there might be more rain. Mama went along to sell her cream and eggs and to buy a few groceries.

Matt's assignment was to stay home with Vonnie and John Paul and to scrub the kitchen floor. Matt didn't mind staying home with the children. John Paul could amuse himself without getting into trouble—he was such a good little kid—and Vonnie would write poetry.

Anyway, Vonnie wasn't speaking to him. Yesterday he had exchanged a pail of lard for her dinner pail and she had hurried off to school, never noticing that the pail was twice as heavy as it should have been. At noon when she opened the pail to get a sandwich, she had stuck her hand in the lard. She had come home from school sputtering.

No, Matt didn't mind staying home with the "little ones." He did mind scrubbing the kitchen floor. It was of plain wooden boards with splinters and there was a week's accumulation of ground-in dirt. He rubbed the planks with ashes, resolving that if the oil well came in, he would buy his mother linoleum for the whole house. Then Vonnie could scrub it.

Feeling self-satisfied for making his mother and Vonnie such a generous gift, Matt took his magazines and climbed up to the hayloft. The hayloft was a comfortable place. He lay by a tiny dust-covered window that let in enough light to read by. The hay was soft and smelled of dust and mice and meadow. Matt finished a story in *Good Housekeeping* about cattle rustlers and then took a little nap. He dreamed of cattle stampeding, but he awoke to the sound of cows bawling to be milked.

What stirred him to action, though, was the rattle of the Model T being driven at top speed down the hard dirt road. It was getting closer and closer. Matt scrambled down the ladder, grabbed a pitchfork, and appeared in the doorway of the barn just as the car turned into the yard. He hoped he looked as though he had been doing chores for the past hour.

"Look at me," John Paul yelled from the back of the barn lot, and while his fascinated family watched, John Paul demonstrated the skill he had been acquiring that afternoon. He took a running start and, with the aid of his pole, sailed smoothly over the feed lot gate.

Pa went over to the gate for a closer look. "What are you using for a pole there?"

The rest of the family gathered around while John Paul

stood in the middle and proudly showed them his pole, smooth, tapered, and about twice as high as he was.

"I sawed one of the shafts off the old buggy. I knew you wouldn't care. That's a very old buggy, and we don't use it very often," he said confidently.

"But we do use it. How can we drive it with one of the shafts gone?" Pa's voice was becoming more and more angry. "You should be spanked."

John Paul stopped smiling. "But Waldo can put it back, can't you, Waldo?"

"What would I use? Flour paste?"

"Can't you put it back?" John Paul's chin began to quiver and his eyes filled with tears.

Everyone began to console him. "That's all right. Don't cry so hard. I will fix it some way. Come see what we brought you from town."

He allowed them to show him the hundred-pound sack of sugar, the canvas for mending the top of the car, and Menno's new heavy work shoes.

Matt went back to his chores thinking about the difference in punishment provided for John Paul's and his own sins. It was not that Matt thought John Paul deserved a spanking. But he had a feeling that if he, Matt, had cut off that buggy shaft, he would have felt the willow switch. This was just one more illustration of the injustice of the world. The poor get poorer, the rich get richer, the good get punished, and the bad get praised.

He was so absorbed with this problem of parental injustice that he let Rosie, the meekest of cows, step into his pail. He saved only a little of the milk by catching the pail quickly. He calmed Rosie by singing to her.

Hallelujah, thine the glory.
Hallelujah, amen.
Hallelujah, thine the glory,
Revive us again.

He went on to milk Hardtail, who was a real challenge because she could knock a milker over with the swish of her tail. Waldo was milking his special pet and problem, Kicker, who had to be hobbled both fore and aft. Even when hobbled, Kicker was a dangerous cow.

Supper that Saturday evening was a celebration. Mama had used some of the sugar to bake a cake, but the main course was *Borscht,* a soup made by a recipe brought over from Russia by the grandparents. It was made of cabbage and other vegetables, including beets which gave it a rich red color, and thickened with heavy cream. Matt was fond of it.

Waldo made a strange request. "Mama, next time you have *Borscht,* could I invite Charlie Boston for supper?"

"Yah, sure. Does Charlie need a good meal?"

Why did Waldo want to have Charlie come for supper? Why get so chummy with an ex-convict? Waldo made no comment and Matt kept his questions to himself.

After supper the older boys went into their bedroom for their Saturday night baths. Pa retired to the front room to read the church paper, *Der Bundesbote,* while Mama gave John Paul his bath in front of the coal burner. Vonnie and Matt were left with the dishes. Vonnie was in poor humor because she had already unbraided her hair, getting ready to wash it, when the chore was assigned. It floated around her shoulders in a crinkled black veil.

"You could have done the dishes by yourself," she

pouted as she stacked the plates. "Or John Paul could have helped."

"John Paul does not wipe dry and the knives and forks get all rusty," Matt reminded her.

Vonnie retorted, "You are an eanmay old umbday eadhay."

Matt had been exposed to pig Latin, and he didn't like being called a dumbhead. "You are an igpay who talks igpay atinlay," he replied and turned his back on her to dip hot water from the reservoir on the back of the stove.

He found himself suddenly blinded. Vonnie had grabbed a molasses pail from the cabinet and turned it over his head. Caught off-guard, he dropped his dipper and grabbed at the molasses pail to lift it off. It was a tight fit.

"Yeow," he yelled. He felt the sharp rim of the pail catch under his ears, and he let it slip back down.

Vonnie gave a taunting laugh, and Matt charged blindly after her to give her the punishment she deserved, not clear in his mind what he would do if he caught her. But of course he couldn't catch her. She could see, and she darted around the kitchen just out of his reach. He stumbled around, bumping into the table and chairs, but he soon knew that he was defeated.

"Matthew! Vonnie!" his father's voice thundered from the front room. "Stop with so much playing around out there."

Matt tried again to maneuver the pail off his head and learned a second dismaying fact. There had been a little molasses left in the bucket and this was now sticking to his hair.

"Waldo, help me," he shouted.

AMERICAN
BEST

"I'll be there as soon as I get my B.V.D.'s on," Waldo called. And he appeared shortly in his clean one-piece suit of underwear. "What's the trouble? Did this little, innocent girl outsmart you again?"

"I just wanted to see how it felt to have a molasses pail pulled down over my head, and now I can't get it off." Matt had been furious for a minute, but his anger had evaporated and he could even feel a faint admiration for his sister. Their games of war and peace were part of life.

Waldo tried to lift the pail off. Vonnie came to help him. "I didn't know there was molasses in the pail," she said, only slightly apologetic. "But then I guess Matt didn't know there was lard in my dinner pail," she added.

"I think what we should do," Waldo said solemnly, "is to stand him on his head and pour hot water into the pail to dissolve the molasses."

While Vonnie reached in and held Matt's ears close to his head, Waldo lifted the pail off.

"Now I'll have to wash my hair," Matt said with disgust, and he took a menacing step toward Vonnie, who flew toward the kitchen door.

She stopped in mid-flight, for she met someone coming in. "Oh, thank you," she said in confusion and stepped back to allow a perfectly strange girl to enter. Immediately behind the stranger Lester followed.

Matt saw that the girl might have been one of the models for the fashion drawings in *Good Housekeeping.* Her pale blonde hair was set in flat waves that curved behind her ears and stopped short. Her dress was of blue silk that fit smoothly. The skirt was fashionably long, ending about six inches above her ankles.

"Gloria, I want you to meet my family. This is Vonnie." Lester introduced his friend in a voice of stern disapproval, and Matt knew that the disapproval was meant for Vonnie and not Gloria. In a lower voice Les said into Vonnie's ear, "Go braid that mop of hair."

"And this is Matt," he continued. "You are a real mess."

"And this is Waldo." Then he hissed, "Go get your clothes on."

They all said, "Hello, Gloria" very politely, except Waldo, who was so overcome with embarrassment that he shot into the bedroom, almost upsetting Menno, who was just coming through the door.

Vonnie disappeared into the front room, but another figure, clad in a flour-sack nightshirt, hurtled through the door to fling himself at Lester's knees. John Paul and Lester fell onto the couch in a tangle of arms and legs. Gloria looked on speechless.

Menno saved the reputation of the family by coming forward to greet her; he was his most shining, handsome and debonair self, and Matt knew that Menno had the situation under control.

Matt went out to the cistern to dunk his molasses head in a pail of water. He doused it several times, but he had no soap and the water was cool. Quickly he dried his head on the roller towel by the washstand. Then he combed his hair at the little mirror, hardly able to see his reflection in the moonlight. He was pleased by the way he was able to get his damp waves to lie down slick and smooth.

When Matt returned to the front room, he found that his parents had been introduced to Gloria, whose last name was Swenson.

Pa furrowed his forehead and said, "Swenson? Is that German?"

"No," Gloria said, not knowing that she had been born to the wrong nationality. "My great-grandparents came from Sweden."

Pa turned to Ma and nodded significantly. *"English."*

"Gloria's father has the farm next to Springers," Lester explained. "I met her while both of us were plowing."

Pa's mouth formed an "O" of surprise. "Plowing?"

"Oh, sure," Gloria said blithely. "We don't have any boys in the family, so I help with lots of the farm work. I like to work outside."

"I invited Gloria to visit us for the weekend. I didn't have a chance to let you know ahead of time. Is it all right, Ma?"

"Of course. She is very welcome," Mama said in careful English. "Let me light a lamp."

Then there was a bustle at the kitchen door, and Mary and Esther walked in. "Surprise! We got the day off and caught a ride home with Karl Berg. Are you glad to see us, Mama?" They kissed her and greeted the rest of the family and were introduced to Gloria.

Then Pa demanded, "How does it happen that you got the Sunday off? You were home last Sunday."

The girls looked at each other, and Mary said, "My people decided that because of the Depression they couldn't afford to pay me ten dollars a week any longer. They asked if I would stay on for five dollars and have every Sunday off. The Hadleys offered Esther the same."

Pa was astonished. "You are going to work for only five dollars a week?"

Esther shrugged. "What should we do? Come home to eat and have you buy our clothes?"

Pa considered this and lost his fight. "Well, I guess something is better than nothing."

Mary turned to Matt. "Whatever did you do to your hair? It looks as though you set it with gooey waving lotion."

"Molasses is cheaper," Menno informed her, running a hand over his own neat black hair with its patent leather shine.

Matt put his hand to his hair and found it stiff and sticky. He glared at Vonnie. "I will have to wash it again."

Mama said, "Mary, get the good sheets from the bottom drawer of the wardrobe. You boys get your blankets and sleep in the barn tonight. Vonnie and Matthew, are the dishes washed?"

Over the dishpans of lukewarm water, Matt confided to Vonnie, "I sure thought she was making *Schputt* when she said she could plow. Did you ever see anybody so dressed up?"

"And such a pretty name."

"If Lester marries her, you'll get used to the name."

Gloria went to church with the family on Sunday. Luckily it was a nice day and they did not have to put the top up, for Waldo had not yet had time to mend it. Luckily, too, Karl Berg happened to drop by as they were piling into the Model T and asked if he could give some of them a ride. Esther got in front with him, and Lester and Gloria climbed into the rumble seat, looking very close together in the small space.

Matt saw that Pa's lips were set in a tight line, and he suspected that Pa didn't like it that Karl had come by. Pa said to Mama as Karl drove off, "I hope he remembers which church they are going to."

Mama tried to smooth his ruffled feathers. "Well, we are crowded in our car. I don't know how we could have got eleven people into it."

"The girls could have driven the buggy," Pa muttered as he climbed into the front seat with Menno and Mama. *"Tjleene Tjinje, tjleene Sorje; Groote Tjinje, groote Sorje* (small children, small sorrows; big children, big sorrows)."

Whatever else he had to say was lost as they exploded out of the driveway. "Menno, slow it down," he commanded, and Menno did.

Matt and Cornie met in the woods that afternoon where they hunted for pawpaws. They found all they wanted and sat down under the Crooked Creek bridge to eat them. Matt thought they were pretty good, once he got used to their mushy texture and slightly nauseating taste.

"That's some good-looking girl Lester drove by with. Are they going to get married?" Cornie asked.

"Not if Pa has any say-so. I heard him tell Ma last night that when he sent Lester to work for Springers, he thought he might take up with one of those plainer Mennonite girls, because Lester is a pretty serious-minded boy, you know. And here he gets sweet on an English girl! But Pa isn't too worried. Les is only twenty and doesn't have any money to get married on. He'll turn his wages over to Pa for at least a year yet."

"My brother Karl is twenty-one."

Matt did not want to talk about Karl and Esther.

"I can't understand why Esther and Lester are willing to give their money to Pa. When I get to be twenty years old, I won't turn my money over to him. I'll run away from home, get a job, and make my own way."

Cornie asked, "Does your Pa need the money?"

"Oh, he has to pay the interest on the mortgage or we lose the place; and he buys feed for the cattle when the pasture is dried up. I know he needs the money, but I don't like to be forced to be bighearted. I hope some day there will be an end to this Depression."

"When your oil well comes in, you won't know there is a Depression."

With that heartening thought, they parted company.

That evening Lester and Gloria caught a ride home with another farmhand from the Prattville community. Karl took Mary and Esther back to their jobs in Tulsa. Matt went to bed with the knowledge that he would be back at the same dull routine the next day.

Mr. Schnell fooled him, though.

Early the next morning as Matt and his mother were out on the back porch getting ready to wash, Ben Voth stopped by. He reported to Mr. Rempel that there was a sign on the door of the Tansy State Bank saying that the bank was closing its doors and that they would remain closed until further notice.

For a moment Matt thought that his father was going to cry, and he was embarrassed and full of pity for him. But the stricken look passed from Pa's face and was replaced by one of anger. "That settles it. Those Republicans! I have made up my mind. I will vote for that Democrat, Roosevelt."

"You can't blame it all on the Republicans," Mr. Voth said mildly. "They say Banker Schnell was in pretty deep with investments. He used the bank's money to make personal investments that didn't pan out, and the examiners caught him."

"Mr. Schnell?" Pa asked in disbelief. "But he is a very good man. He wouldn't do anything dishonest."

"I only know what the bank examiners are saying. I have to be on my way." Mr. Voth got into his car. "If they don't get robbed, they get busted, I always say. I think I'll put my money in a sock under the mattress from now on." He drove off with a wave.

Mama had been a silent onlooker during their conversation. She turned to go back into the house. "Now we won't have to worry about how to spend the lease money." That was her only comment about the whole affair of the oil lease.

Pa turned to Matt. "There, you see. An educated man, and crooked as a hairpin. Don't talk to me about high school ever again."

He stalked off toward the barn, and Matt went back to the washboard.

"Looks like I'll grow up to be a washerwoman," he grumbled when his mother brought him the lye soap.

She turned out the pockets of a pair of dirty overalls. "Don't give up yet. Just keep praying about your needs and keep reading your books and magazines."

"A praying washerwoman," Matt muttered, "old and gray and well-read." He rubbed the soiled collar of his father's shirt on the washboard, applying lye soap, elbow grease, and lots of strong feeling.

10
Matt Joins the Church

The month of October is the best month of the year, Matt decided as he threw his line into the Verdigris River. The grasshopper he was using for bait soon attracted a big catfish and Matt pulled it in. Fishing was fine, but the weather was much too dry. The fencerows flamed with sumac, and the leaves of the blackjack were already gold.

This was good baseball weather, too, but the World Series was over for the year. The New York Yankees had won the pennant, beating the Chicago Cubs in four straight games. Interesting events were going on all over the country. The new Rockefeller Center in New York City was being played up by the paper, and so was the Chicago World's Fair that was to open the next summer. There were some bright spots in the country, even with the Depression and the drought.

Politics interested Matt. He read everything he could find about the presidential campaign, which just now was going strong. Pa had Matt read articles from the papers so that he could make up his mind whom to vote for. Pa said that he would probably vote for Roosevelt, but that he would change his mind and vote for the Republicans' President Hoover if he could see one encouraging sign of a return to prosperity. His confidence in banks was completely gone. The Tansy Bank had closed its doors for good, and Mr. Schnell had moved away.

Pa still was bewildered by the failure of the Tansy Bank. "I thought he was using the bank's money to make his investments. I knew the bank was buying up land and Mr. Schnell told me himself he was investing the bank's money in some good stock. But I didn't know he was using *my* money."

Matt tried to help him. "Don't you see, Pa, the bank's money was your money and everybody else's who deposited it there. He was using your money. What the examiners don't know yet is whether he was doing something criminal or not."

"They should have put my money in a pile by itself and let nobody but me use it." With this statement Pa considered the argument closed.

Matt pulled in his line and looked at the sun. The days were growing shorter. It was time to start for home if he wanted to do the milking before dark. With his string of catfish in one hand and his pole in the other, he urged Jerry toward home.

The work at home was heavier now that Menno was gone. Everyone was surprised, including Menno, by his new job. Nancy John Yoder had stopped Pa in town one day to ask if he had a boy who might work for him, doing his chores and feeding his cattle and hogs. The work was too heavy for his girls, he felt, but he couldn't afford to pay more than board and twenty dollars a month with

Sundays off. Payment could be in corn and oats if Pa wanted that.

Pa had accepted for Menno, and Menno had accepted for himself, although he complained that he would be making about ten cents an hour. Still, this was better than nothing and Pa wouldn't have to feed him.

"But that job sure won't give me much spending money. How can I ever save enough to buy a little car?" he complained. "How can I make an impression on those Tansy girls if I don't have a car? They are just sitting at home breathless, waiting for me to take them roller skating or to the high school ball games."

Matt could tell that Pa didn't quite know how to take this banter from his gay son.

"You will be glad to take one of our Mennonite girls out after you spend the winter with these plain Amish women," Pa predicted hopefully.

Menno laughed. "My taste in girls doesn't run to long-faced, long-haired, long-skirted Amish girls." He went to pack a box of his clothes. Matt noticed that he took along his good suit.

Menno had gone riding away in Yoder's buggy. Pa had offered to deliver him to the Yoder farm, but Mr. Yoder said he would be passing by anyway. Menno was not at all embarrassed to be driving in a buggy, as Mary and Esther would have been. In fact, he seemed to enjoy sitting there behind the high-stepping sorrels.

Matt missed Menno more than he would admit. His brother had added some spice to the routine of chores, even though he could make a peace-loving brother mad enough to go to war. Actually, Matt had expected Waldo to miss Menno more than he did. But Waldo had taken more and more of an interest in Charlie Boston. Even though Charlie was five years older, the two of them seemed to hit it off uncommonly well. Waldo was showing him how to do things around the farm and they had great plans for a trapping season. Ruefully Matt had to admit that the more he saw of Charlie, the more Charlie seemed like a farm boy and less like a bank robber.

Matt reached his own yard and, giving Jerry a slap to send him toward the barn, hurried to get the chores done since there was church that night. A visiting evangelist, Reverend Temple, was starting two weeks of revival meetings at the Zion Church.

There would, in fact, be two sermons every night, one in German by the regular minister and one in English by the evangelist. It would be the evangelist's task to bring the backsliders back to the church and to gather new converts into the fellowship. Matt knew that he was expected to go forward this year, and he supposed he would.

On the first night of the revival, the church was comfortably filled, although the crowd would be larger on a Sunday morning. Some people would wait to see if the speaker was a good one before they decided to come.

Pa deplored this attitude. "The Rempels go to church because there is church; when there is church, a good Mennonite goes."

The song leader announced the song and the accompanist took her place at the reed organ. The song was in German, *"O dass ich tausend Zungen haette"* (O, That I Had a Thousand Voices); and the congregation sang as though they did, through all nine verses.

After the opening prayer, Reverend Reimer gave his German sermon. Matt listened, but listening to High German was more difficult than singing it. He looked forward to hearing the English visitor. He wanted to learn, during these two weeks of sermons, whether he was ready to join the church.

The evangelist went around to the various homes for meals. He came to the Rempels for dinner one day soon after the services began.

When the meal was over, Matt went out to the barn. Reverend Temple found him there a half-hour later forking clean hay into the stalls. The evangelist wanted to talk to him, he said, about his soul.

"I hope you will feel ready to come forward next Friday. You want salvation, don't you? You know that you can be saved only by trusting Jesus, don't you?" Reverend Temple spoke gently.

Matt had been hearing these phrases all his life, and he knew that he did want salvation. He wanted to be saved from sin, to be a Christian, to belong to the church. But he had questions. Right now all he could say to Reverend Temple was, "Sure, I want to be saved." But after the evangelist left and Matt went back to the work of cleaning out the stalls, he kept asking himself, "What does it all mean? How do I know I'm saved?"

During the nights that followed, Reverend Temple preached mightily and several people came forward, but it seemed that the revival was not the success that it had been in other years. Matt's parents agreed that the preacher was "feeding the flock" rather than "finding lost lambs," and this was important, too.

On Thursday night of the second week, however, there was one new convert who surprised the Zion Church and provided conversation for years to come. When Reverend Temple asked for the lost souls to come forward, Charlie Boston went hesitantly up the aisle to the altar. Matt was the most surprised onlooker of all. He hadn't even known that Charlie was there.

Waldo went up afterward to shake Charlie's hand and Matt heard Charlie's explanation: "I know I done some wrong things and I want to make things right. I never joined no church before, but I just decided it was time I did. And I wanted to join your church," he added to Waldo.

Was this Pretty Boy Floyd joining church? But the Zion Church welcomed Charlie as a true penitent.

Friday night was the last night of the revival, and Matt's Sunday school class had been asked to sit together near the front. There were six girls and Matt and an older boy. Their Sunday school teacher sat with them. After the sermon, a hymn was sung softly by the congregation, a song from the English hymnbook, "Just as I Am, Without One Plea." This was an invitation hymn, inviting people to come forward.

The congregation sang a stanza. Then the preacher quietly urged the sinners to come forward. "Your Lord and Savior is not willing that anyone should perish. Repent now. Now is the acceptable time. Not tomorrow or next year, but tonight."

None of the class made a move to go forward, and Matt didn't feel it was up to him to go. He wasn't even sure he wanted to go. Maybe next year would be a better time.

Then the congregation sang "Softly and Tenderly Jesus is Calling." Matt felt that every mind in the congregation was willing him to get up and go forward, but he still didn't feel that he should. Was his heart right with God? He didn't know. And the evangelist said that this was the last invitation. "Don't let this opportunity go by. You don't know when your time on earth will be up. Maybe you will die in your bed tonight."

Matt had often thought of the "uncertainty of life," as the minister called it, and he knew that he wanted to die a Christian. But he rebelled against the idea of going forward just to save his soul at the last minute before death. Was that the way God wanted his soul, frightened into salvation? The pulse in his temples pounded and his hands were sticky with sweat. He decided at that moment to wait until next year when things might be more clear in his mind.

The congregation came to the last verse. Suddenly the Sunday school teacher stood up and leaned over to speak to Vera Voth. "Don't you want to go forward and say that you accept Jesus Christ as your Lord and Savior?" he said aloud so that everyone in the row could hear.

Vera rose and the teacher stood back to let her pass. As she went forward, everyone in the class also rose and followed. Matt felt he couldn't sit there by himself, and he joined the procession. It was a good step to take, he was sure of that. At the same time he was angry with himself for doing what he had decided not to do.

Afterward, the church people gathered around to shake hands with the new converts. His mother kissed him and wiped a few tears from her eyes, and Matt felt deeply moved, for she seldom kissed him. He knew that his going forward was important to his parents, and he was glad that he had pleased them.

Reverend Temple left the next day, but Sunday would be an important day because the new converts would be baptized and take Communion with the rest of the congregation.

The baptismal service was performed first. Matt lined up with the other candidates at the front of the church and knelt before the minister. The minister asked them whether they were willing "to become members of the body of Christ," and each answered for himself. Then the minister sprinkled each of them from a bowl of water, "in the name of the Father, the Son, and the Holy Ghost." Matt was now a member of the Zion Mennonite Church. But he had a feeling that God was looking down on him and saying, "Matt, I know you are bluffing. You don't really belong with this group."

Communion followed baptism. Now that these new converts were full-fledged members of the church, they could take their first Communion.

Matt thought that the words of the service were beautiful, and the minister read them reverently.

"And he took the bread and brake it and said, 'Do this in remembrance of me.' "

The deacons passed around the plate of bread which had been broken into pieces. Then they passed around a glassful of grape juice, and every member took a sip. They were symbols of the broken body and spilled blood of Christ.

The minister next read the story of how Jesus washed the disciples' feet, and the people went by small groups into the little rooms for the foot washing ceremony, the women on one side and the men on the other. The older people went first.

Matt was a little fearful about the foot washing part of the Communion service. He had watched the rest of the congregation take Communion often enough, but foot washing always took place in the little rooms off the entry. His brothers had told him how it was done. He knew that it was a symbolic ceremony, that the purpose was not to wash feet to get them clean. In fact, his mother had admonished the boys to wash their feet carefully the night before Communion. She didn't want anyone to have to wash dirty Rempel feet.

When finally it came his turn, Matt went self-consciously into the anteroom and waited while two of the older boys finished using the basin.

As things worked out, Charlie Boston was his partner. Matt sat in the chair while Charlie dipped water over first one foot and wiped it, and then the other foot. Matt did the same for Charlie, and they finished by exchanging the holy kiss on the cheek.

All during the ceremony, Matt tried hard to remember the significance of it. Jesus had done this for his disciples to show that no man is better than his brother, that no one is too good to do an act of kindness to another, but the details of the actual foot washing kept intruding. It was hard to keep solemn when Charlie splashed too much water and when the coarse towel tickled his foot. The holy kiss seemed awkward. Men didn't go around kissing in this day and age.

Matt wished he had had a partner other than Charlie.

JAN GLEYSTEEN

He was not sure that Charlie was really sincere in his decision to join the church. Perhaps he was doing this to cover his true character. "I don't know if Charlie Boston should be in the church with us true believers," Matt thought as he went back to his place after the foot washing.

Then he caught himself up short. He was doing the opposite of the commandment that Jesus gave about washing each other's feet. Here he was, thinking that he was better than Charlie Boston. Matt guessed that he hadn't changed a lot when he went forward to join the church.

That afternoon Matt compared notes with Cornie as they explored the bright woods along the Verdigris.

"You folks do it the easy way," Cornie commented. "I was baptized last spring, and we were dunked—I mean immersed—three times. You know you've been baptized when you go under that cold water backward three times."

Matt defended his church. "I don't think you have to get wet all over to let God know that you are willing to join church. It is the idea that is important."

"I want to make sure I'm doing all I can to be a good Christian. My cousins over at Haley belong to another branch of the church, and they say you have to be immersed forward and that we are not really saved because we were immersed backward. I asked our preacher to do me both ways, but he wouldn't listen."

"If you want a strict church, you should join the Amish," Matt suggested. "Menno says the Amish are so strict they can't do anything without getting into trouble. The only place they can go is to church."

"I'll bet Menno has a hard time with the Amish, the way he likes to run around."

"Oh, he likes them. He says they are very serious and sincere and hard working. He says the Yoder girls are pretty in a plain way. What does he mean by that?"

Without trying to answer that question, Cornie said, "Did you know that my brother Karl took your sister Esther back to her job in Tulsy after church Sunday night?"

"Why would he want to do a thing like that? Pa won't like it." As soon as he had said the words, Matt wished he had kept his mouth shut.

"Why not?" Cornie bristled. "Karl is as good as that Bill Jantz that Mary likes."

"Well, Pa wants Esther to go with boys from our church."

"You should hear my pa! He doesn't want the boys to marry girls who have not been baptized proper."

"If my sister isn't good enough for your brother, then I guess I'm not good enough for you to hang around with. I'll just go on home." Matt turned his back on Cornelius Berg.

"Well, if you can't hear the truth, I guess there is nothing I can do about it."

They parted company.

A quarrel with Cornie was always depressing, but it was not the first disagreement they had had on the subject of church.

Surprisingly, Pa was the one to lift Matt's depression. After supper he came to sit beside Matt in front of the glowing coal burner. "You are going to be a good Mennonite now, since you joined the church, yah? No fighting, no running around; Menno, he runs around too much. You will be more like Lester, serious about the church,

but you don't want to marry an English girl. Understand?"

"Yes, Pa."

"No running around, remember the German, read the Bible."

"Yes, Pa."

"You are a good boy, Matthew, and if times get better, maybe you can go to high school. You learn so many good things from your books, I have changed my mind. Maybe schooling is good. Is that what you want me to say?"

"Yes, Pa!"

"Just one thing. It depends on how Grandpa Enns feels about this. You can't go to school if Grandpa says school is wrong. Understand?"

"Sure, Pa, I understand."

"All right. Now you go help Mama with the supper dishes."

Matt flew to the kitchen and took the dishrag from his mother's hand. "Shoo. You go into the front room and rest with Pa. I will do the dishes myself."

She laughed. "My, my. Is this what baptism does for a boy?" But she went to join Pa in the parlor.

Matt's high spirits lasted as long as the soapsuds. Because Pa thought Matt was a "good" boy, he was going to let him go to school. Pa didn't know that he had joined the church unwillingly. Matt felt that somehow he had been dishonest.

"But I don't care. If Pa says I can go to school, I will go. He doesn't have to know that I never intended to join the church. Now if I can find some money, all my problems will be solved."

He didn't feel nearly as glad about the situation as he should have. It seemed to be just another example of his lack of courage. He didn't have the courage to be honest any more than he had the courage to face physical danger. He was a real *Taugenichts,* a worth-nothing.

The thought occurred to him that Charlie, even with his prison record, might be a better church member than he was, but Matt quickly put that idea out of his mind.

11
Trouble for Charlie Boston

On a rainy Saturday afternoon in November, Vonnie and John Paul were shooed out of the house by their mother. Vonnie had been skipping rope in a frenzy of motion, although she did not have a rope. John Paul had attempted the standing broad jump over Vonnie's cot.

"You have too much energy for this little house. Go work it off in the barn," Mama had commanded with unusual firmness.

They had no trouble amusing themselves there in the company of Donald the goat. They climbed up the ladder into the mow, caught hold of a rope, and swung themselves out over the open driveway that ran through the center of the barn. Then they got the idea of piling hay in the driveway and dropping from the swinging rope into the hay. Even Matt found this to be good fun, and he left his job of cleaning stalls on the other side of the barn to play for a few minutes.

The Model T was parked in the driveway. It was closed up tight with the mended top up and its side curtains snapped on since the weather was cold and the rain was likely to continue. Vonnie had dusted it only that morning in preparation for the clean clothes that would ride to church in it on Sunday.

The three were resting, lying on their backs in the hay in the driveway, panting from the effort of climbing up the ladder time after time.

"Look at Donald," John Paul called, peering up into the dimness of the haymow. "How did he get up there in the mow?"

Matt looked up from his nest in the hay. "He must have some mountain goat for an ancestor and thinks he is in the Alps."

Vonnie went to sit on the running board of the car. "Here Donald," she called softly. "Don't be afraid. Come on, honey, just jump back into the hay. You won't get hurt."

Donald looked down on all of them, obviously unafraid. Gathering his feet together, he jumped with all the grace and daintiness of a ballet-dancing mountain goat. However, he aimed not for the hay pile but for his good friend Vonnie. He landed squarely on top of the Model T. His weight was too much for the canvas top, and he crashed through. Matt rushed to open the car door for a bewildered Donald, who scrambled out of the car and vanished to the other side of the barn.

The three of them stood silently looking at the tattered top. "Well, we can't get it fixed in time for church tomorrow," Matt said.

"Maybe the weather will clear up and we won't need the top," John Paul said hopefully.

Vonnie had a practical suggestion. "Let's not tell anybody about it until tomorrow when we see what the weather is like. Pa will take it better on a nice day than on a rainy day."

This seemed a sensible, though cowardly, way of handling the situation. Matt went back to his work and Vonnie and John Paul went to the house. Neither Pa nor Waldo had any occasion to go looking at the car the rest of the day. The rain continued, slow but soaking.

Matt spent a restless night, for the thought of what his father would say kept nagging at his dreams. Once he awoke to hear Spud barking furiously, but he went back to his dream of chasing a goat all over the house.

At breakfast that morning it was still raining when Pa said, "It is good that our car is snug and tight. I don't want Mama to get her fancy bonnet wet."

Matt looked at Vonnie and John Paul, and all three looked down into their oatmeal. Then John Paul said, "We wouldn't get wet if there was a hole only in the middle," but Vonnie kicked him under the table and he ended his speech holding his ankle and saying, "Alas, alas." John Paul tried to find occasions to use words he was learning in his second grade reader.

Vonnie hissed, "You are a *Glummskopp.*"

When everyone was ready for church, Waldo went to back the car out of the barn and bring it around to the front door so they could get in without getting wet. Matt, Vonnie, and John Paul watched from the kitchen window as Waldo heaved back the sliding doors of the barn and then stopped in the doorway to stare inside. They saw him turn to run back to the house, his face showing surprise and disbelief. They turned together to watch him burst into the kitchen.

"Pa, the car! It isn't there. It's been stolen."

In unison, the three youngest Rempels let out a long breath.

Pa had been sitting at the table reading his Sunday school lesson, but he jumped to his feet. "No. You are making *Schputt.* Who would want to steal our car? Maybe you forgot where you put it."

"It's been in the barn all week. It isn't there now."

All of them had to go out in the rain to stand in the doorway of the barn to look at the spot where the car had stood and to declare that it was, indeed, gone.

"I heard Spud barking last night," Matt offered.

And then all of them remembered that they had heard Spud barking. Why hadn't they heard the car being started? When you cranked it, it made as much noise as a threshing machine until you got it throttled down.

"I have heard that car thieves push them out of the barn and down the road so you can't hear them," Waldo said. "But why would they steal our old Lizzie? There's a better car in every barn around here."

That was a mystery that no one had any theories about.

"Well, harness the horses to the spring wagon," Pa ordered. "We have to get to church, even if we get there late."

So they arrived at church late and wet, but they dried out in front of a good fire, after the service. The theft of the Rempel car was a good topic for conversation and kept the congregation at church half an hour longer than usual. The neighbors took them back home after church, leaving Waldo to bring back the team and wagon.

Early Monday morning Ben Voth took Pa to the county

seat to report the theft to the sheriff. About ten o'clock the sheriff came driving into the yard in his black county sedan followed by his deputy driving the Rempels' Model T. All the Rempel family gathered in the yard to inspect their returned possession.

"Here you are, Pete," the sheriff hailed Pa as he stepped from his car. "We found it ten miles east of here in a field. They ran it till it was out of gas and left it. All I can see wrong with it is the hole in the top."

"Looks like they stopped awful sudden and one of 'em flew through the top," the deputy offered with a laugh. "We should go look for a man with canvas sticking out of his ears."

The sheriff and his deputy left with the thanks of the Rempel family. Matt had wished for a moment that the car would be so badly damaged that they would have had to get a new one, but Pa soon corrected that idea. "We are sure lucky to have this car back. I don't know where we would ever get the money to buy a new one."

Even a 1925 Model T was better than no car at all.

"See how much gas is in her and put her in the barn," Pa commanded and went back to his work.

Matt was proud to take care of the car. He cranked it up and drove it over to the gas barrel. He had to take the front seat out to get to the gas tank, and when he did, he found a small silver pocketknife under the seat. He recognized it immediately as Windy John's. But Windy John had never ridden in this car. Could it have been his nephew, Charlie Boston? If Charlie had stolen the car, what use had he made of it? Was he merely joyriding on a rainy night?

If Charlie Boston was really Charles "Pretty Boy" Floyd, he wouldn't have borrowed a car to go joyriding. He would have used it as a getaway car or for an emergency. But why steal a car from the farm next door to where he lived, an old one at that, and take it ten miles east and then come home again to Windy John's place? Or had he come back?

Matt realized that the facts he had did not make sense in the way he was putting them together. He kept mulling them over. If Charlie Boston was really Pretty Boy Floyd . . . .

When the *Tulsa Tribune* came in the noon mail, Matt was the first to get at it. He looked for all mention of bank robberies. There was no new one, only an editorial mentioning that there had been forty-four robberies in the state of Oklahoma that year up to November 1, but there had not been one that day. Then Matt realized that the paper was a day late to rural subscribers, and if there had been a robbery Saturday afternoon, it would not be in the paper. He wouldn't know until tomorrow's paper.

That afternoon he begged for an hour off to go over to Cornie's, and his father gave him permission. He found Cornie in the barn, playing with a nest of kittens. Cornie jumped to his feet, but when he saw that it was Matt and not his father, he settled down in the hay again.

"What brings you over? Did you discover oil?"

"Nope. But did you hear about our car being stolen?" This time Matt had something that made old Cornie's eyes bug out. And after he told him all the details, Matt asked, "Did you hear of any bank robberies Saturday? Could these guys have robbed a bank and had bad luck with their car, then laid low until they could steal a car?"

Cornie looked at him with astonishment. "Sure, there was a bank robbery, but not a very big one. Over to Spencer. I didn't even know they had a bank there, but the radio said they got eight hundred dollars from it and vanished without a trace."

"But Spencer is west of here and our car was found east."

"Maybe Pretty Boy was headed out to the Cookson Hills again. That's where he hides out."

"Not if Pretty Boy is hiding out at Windy John's," Matt thought, but he didn't tell Cornie of the knife or of his suspicions of Charlie Boston.

"Say, Matt," Cornie asked, "do you think this is the answer to your prayers? If you could collect that three thousand dollars for the capture of that bank robber, you would be sitting as pretty as Pretty Boy."

Matt had not let himself think about the three thousand dollars, and now he answered casually, "Even if it was Pretty Boy, I don't know how I could catch him."

Matt went home then, knowing he would have to milk the cows in the dark if he didn't get to it.

That night while Matt and the two younger children were doing dishes, Vonnie laughed. "I'll just bet those car robbers were surprised when they got in the car and found that the rain was coming through."

For the first time since Sunday morning, Matt remembered Donald's accident. "Say, we never did tell Pa about that. We have to tell him."

"We do?" Vonnie was doubtful. "I thought maybe this was the way God answered my prayer that I wouldn't get spanked for what Donald did."

Matt shook his head. "I don't think God would go to all that trouble to save you a spanking."

John Paul was philosophical. "Well, since God let the car be stolen, he let it be stolen on the right night."

Before they went to bed, they told their father how Donald had jumped through the car top. He looked over the top of his paper at them. "That dumb goat," he said with a growl, and went back to his headlines.

Mama paused over the sock she was darning. "I hope Waldo has the patience to fix the top again."

The next morning Matt found it possible to visit Windy John on the excuse that he wanted to see how the oil well was working. He found Windy John in the barn mending harness.

"How are you, Mr. Boston?" Matt asked.

"Better."

"Were you poorly?"

"Oh, that rainy weather is hard on my bad leg. Seems to make the bunion hurt on the foot I lost."

This was an idea beyond understanding to Matt, and Windy John said he couldn't explain the reason. That was just the way it was.

"How's Charlie?"

"He's got a terrible cold."

"How'd he come to catch cold?"

"I don't rightly know. He was fine when he went to bed, but the next morning he had a fever and this cold."

Matt didn't know how far he should go with this, but he had to know one more answer. "What night was that?"

Windy John straightened up to look at him curiously. "Seems to me you are mighty interested in poor Charlie's cold. Can't a boy have a simple little head cold like anybody else?"

Matt said hastily, "No offense, Mr. Boston. Seems like everybody has a cold with this weather. Here, I found something of yours." He extended the silver knife.

"Why, thank you. I didn't know I lost it, but I'm mighty glad to get it back. Where was it?"

Matt thought quickly. He didn't know how much he should tell. Windy John didn't seem to have anything to hide; he seemed really surprised to see the knife. "I just found it."

"Now I remember. Charlie borrowed it the other day to trim his fingernails. I guess he forgot to give it back to me and dropped it someplace."

Matt tried to absorb this information without showing his excitement.

"Well, good-bye, Mr. Boston. I hope Charlie gets better in a hurry. I have to get home now."

Matt had learned one thing: Charlie had a cold, which he undoubtedly caught sitting in the rain in the Rempel car. Did Windy John know about Charlie's midnight joyride? Probably not. What was the next step to take if he was going to capture Pretty Boy Floyd and win three thousand dollars?

That afternoon Matt decided that the only thing to do was to confide in his father. Pa listened to the evidence, but he was skeptical. "I don't see how Windy John's Charlie could be Pretty Boy Floyd. He isn't the smart-aleck type that Floyd is. In fact, he seems like a nice, quiet boy. But that pocketknife is a riddle. I think we should go see the sheriff about it."

In the county seat they were surprised to find the town full of people, almost as though it were a Saturday.

"I forgot about this being election day," Pa said.

Matt nodded. "It's the local primaries," he said. "Aren't you going to vote, Pa?"

"No. I have never voted and I never will, although I want you to know that I am a good Republican."

"But you were always talking about how you were going to vote for Roosevelt if things didn't get better," Matt persisted.

Matt had learned at school that it was his duty to vote, and he knew that some of the younger church members did vote, but he didn't tell his father that.

His father looked a little sheepish. "That was just talk. Mennonites don't vote. We don't believe in having anything to do with the government."

A loudspeaker was playing "Happy Days Are Here Again," the Democrats' theme song, and Matt could almost believe it. The record played over and over. What was the Republicans' theme song? Where were all those Republicans who had helped elect Hoover back in 1928?

They went into the county jail to tell their story to the sheriff.

The sheriff listened, then reached for his Stetson and said, "I'll just go out there and talk to Charlie a little and see what I can find out. Nobody by the name of Charlie Boston in my files, though."

"Boston isn't his real name," Matt said. "He has a record, but I don't know what his name is."

The Rempels went back to the farm. "We did our duty by the law," Pa said. "Now I don't want to be mixed up in it anymore. Mennonites should stay clear of the law."

Matt's curiosity was almost more than he could stand for the rest of the afternoon, but nothing happened. The best that could have happened was for the sheriff to come by to offer him a three-thousand-dollar check, but that didn't happen either. It was not until after supper that a knock came on the kitchen door and Matt opened it to find Windy John.

"Your pa home?"

"Sure. Come in, Mr. Boston."

Pa came into the kitchen and greeted Windy John and gave him a chair at the kitchen table.

"I came to offer you folks my apologies," Windy John began. "I misrepresented Charlie to you as my nephew, and he ain't really no kin of mine at all."

Pa said, "Well, I guess there is no harm in that. Though I don't see why you should let on like he was your relation."

Windy John leaned his elbows on the table and told Pa the facts that he had told Matt about Charlie having asked him for work when he got out of reform school. "He was good help, too. Paid attention to business. But the sheriff came this afternoon and asked him if he had anything to do with stealing your car, and he confessed that he had driven it away."

Pa said, "I had an idea he was mixed up with it."

"I hope you don't judge the boy too hard. I've come to think of him as my kin, and I hate to see things go against him. It happened like this. These pals he had in reform school come around late Saturday night. They had robbed the Spencer bank, but their car got stuck on a back road. So they hiked over to my place to see Charlie. How they knew where he was I don't know, but those things get around, even though Charlie tried to lay low. They got him out to talk to them, and then at gunpoint they had him find the nearest car and drive them away. When they ran out of gas, they started walkin' and let Charlie come on home."

"I'm real sorry about Charlie," Pa said. "They won't put him back, will they?"

"The sheriff took him to town to see what information he could get about these boys, but he talked like they would let Charlie come back. Of course, now everybody will know that he is an ex-convict."

"Not if none of us say anything," Pa promised. "The sheriff won't talk if we ask him not to."

"Were these other guys wanted by the police?" Matt asked, glad for Charlie that he wasn't Pretty Boy, but sorry to see his three thousand dollars fly up the chimney.

"Oh, they are wanted all right. The sheriff thought they had pulled five robberies. But they ain't big-time stuff like Pretty Boy Floyd."

"Wasn't one of them named Charlie?" Matt asked.

"Naw," Windy John said in disgust. "They like to call each other Charlie because their hero is Pretty Boy. The sheriff says Floyd ain't robbed a bank for quite a while now. He is stayin' close to his farm over in the Cooksons."

Windy John took his leave, and the Rempel family sat around the kitchen table to marvel over the news. They were all willing to give Matt credit for figuring things out. It might even be that the bank robbers would be caught because of Matt's figuring. Matt didn't tell them that his original hunch about Pretty Boy Floyd had been wrong.

He felt a vague regret about the whole affair. He had missed another opportunity to show his courage. He was not sure just how or where he should have been brave. Should he have gone out to the barn that night when he heard Spud barking? He couldn't run after Spud every time he barked, though. Should he have confronted Charlie Boston himself rather than taking the matter to the sheriff? No. This had been a job for the authorities.

The bank robbers were caught a week later, thanks to the information Charlie had given the sheriff. They confessed to having robbed the Wellington bank, Matt was interested to learn. Charlie was cleared, and the sheriff let him return to Windy John's custody.

That was the end of the Charlie affair, and it was also the end of Donald, as far as the Rempels were concerned. Pa took him to the next farm sale and traded him for three cans of gooseberries. Vonnie bore up very well with the loss of her favorite pet until Mama served the gooseberries in a pie. "I feel that we are eating Donald," Vonnie wailed and rushed from the table.

God had not answered his prayer by helping him win the three-thousand-dollar reward. But Matt believed that God answered prayers, and he became more and more convinced that the prayer would be answered in the form of an oil well. He hoped his patience would hold out until the oil well could be brought in.

12
A Doodlebug for Rempel No. 1

The presidential election interested Matt. He read all he could find in the newspaper and in the *Literary Digest*s that Mary brought home. He discussed the candidates and their programs with Pa, trying to find words in the Low German for ideas like stock market, balanced budget, and unemployment relief. Their talk soon became a mixture of Low German and English.

"Roosevelt says the Smoot-Hawley tariff is not helping the farmers. The farm dollar is worth half what it was before the war. The farmer has to have the same chance as everybody else," Matt argued.

Pa tried to defend Hoover when he could. "The President believes that the farmer needs a protective tariff on farm products." Then he gave Matt a sharp look. "Are you planning to be a politician?"

"No, but I like to read about such things."

"I wonder if Hoover will win the election?" Pa asked.

Matt reported that the *Literary Digest* straw vote said that Roosevelt would win by a landslide. He read this after the election but before the final vote was in and counted.

"But this article says that General Atterbury, president of the Pennsylvania Railroad, Calvin Coolidge, former president of the United States, and Henry Ford, of Ford Motor Company, were campaigning for Hoover."

The magic name of Henry Ford shook Pa a little. "You say Henry Ford told the workers to vote for Hoover? Now there is a sensible man. He must know what he is saying."

In spite of Atterbury, Coolidge, and Ford, Roosevelt won the 1932 election in which he carried forty-two states to Hoover's six.

Matt looked at all the cartoons in the paper which proclaimed that "prosperity is just around the corner," and felt with the rest of the country that the Depression was bound to disappear right away now that Roosevelt was elected, even though he would not take office until March.

The political situation interested Matt, but there was a more exciting prospect closer to home. Finally the Company was making motions to drill an oil well on the Rempel property. This well would gush forth to solve all their problems. Who needed the Democrats? Who needed banks? From now on they would carry their cash around in gunny sacks.

The family discussed it at every meal. "First we will buy a Delco plant that makes electricity," Waldo suggested. "Then we can get all kinds of things that will help with the work. We could have a mill for grinding feed, a bathroom for the house, an electric iron for Matt, and all kinds of things for Ma."

"I could do with a washing machine, and it wouldn't have to be electric," Mama said. "One of those with a gasoline engine would be nice."

Pa got up from the table and stopped behind her chair, laying his hand on her shoulder. "For Mama we will buy a new house, with linoleum on the floor and enough bedrooms so that only two will have to sleep in a room. What do you say to that, Mama? And a nice dress, yah?"

"Only a dream," Mama reminded him. "God hasn't promised us an oil well."

"John Paul, what do you want to buy with the oil well?" Vonnie asked.

"A baseball glove," John Paul replied, scooping up the last of his oatmeal.

"I want a doll with hair. What do you want, Matt?"

"Everybody knows what I want," Matt said gruffly and got up to leave the table.

Out on the back porch he dreamed his old dreams. Going to Tansy to the high school, maybe driving the car or at least riding Beauty. Sitting in class, answering questions, writing themes, working with other kids on his geometry, reading the stories in the literature books. All this depended on the oil well.

"God, you know how much I want to go to school. If it is your will, let the oil well come in. We don't need to be rich, God. Just enough so that I can go to school and Mama can have her gasoline washer."

The Company didn't dawdle around with this one. The seismologist had a feeling that there was a good pool in this country and he was working hard to find it.

He explained about oil to Matt one afternoon. "We talk about a pool, but you shouldn't think of the oil as lying in a pool down there under the ground. It is in porous rocks, and these rocks are as hard as the stone used to build your courthouse. We talk about oil sands, but here, too, we mean sandstone, and don't let anybody hit you on the head with a piece of sandstone."

"Then what makes the oil flow out of that rock?" Matt asked as he watched Mr. Capley fold up his charts.

"The tremendous pressure forces it up. The pressure may be from water or gas that is also present."

The Company bought leases on several farms around, and they planned to give full attention to the area. They were putting in wells on the Voth and Schmidt places at the same time.

Matt had a feeling that the Rempel farm was going to be the winner. He just felt lucky, and he went around singing "Happy Days Are Here Again" until his mother cautioned, "Don't get your hopes too high. It just may be that we don't have oil. That field grows good corn, you know."

"Oh, Ma. You just don't know what to do with money and you are afraid of it. Don't worry. We'll all get used to it."

There was disagreement about where to do the drilling.

Pa had asked Windy John to doodlebug with his peach twig. John had gone over certain sections of the cornfield and reported that he didn't get a clear signal. Matt was disappointed by this report, but then he didn't really believe in doodlebugging, anyway, and the Company ought to know what it was doing.

Then an independent character arrived from Tulsa. Greasy Galt drove up in a rattletrap truck one day, before the crew arrived for earnest work, to ask Pa if he would allow him to predict exactly where the oil was to be found.

"I'm president of the Never Miss Petroleum Finding Company, and for a small fee I will tell you exactly where to dig."

Pa stuck his thumb under his overall strap and gave the newcomer a good looking over. Matt was more amused than impressed by what he saw. Greasy Galt, who said he got his nickname because he had found so many oil wells for the big companies, was short and red-haired. His truck was piled high with paraphernalia.

Pa said finally, "The Company will decide where to dig. You're welcome to try your rig out there in my cornfield, but I won't pay you any money."

Matt was disappointed. He wanted to see what all the gadgets in the truck were for.

"Tell you what I'll do," Mr. Galt said brightly. "I'll give you my services free of charge. I just want you to get the best well possible, and I am willing to give you the benefit of my knowledge just for the joy of helping out a fellow human being. Now where is the field?"

Pa told Matt to show Mr. Galt where the Company was planning to drill. Matt jumped on the running board of the truck, and they rattled out to the cornfield. Mr. Galt started pulling the machinery from his truck and assembling his gear. The basis of the contraption was a wheelbarrow on which was fixed an array of wooden branches. The tips of the branches were covered with copper, which, said Mr. Galt, made them more sensitive to oil than just a plain old unadorned branch. Furthermore, these were willow branches.

By the time he had the wheelbarrow ready to wheel, he had quite an audience. Windy John and Charlie had

arrived, and some of the crew from the Company were standing around waiting for action.

Greasy Galt appeared unimpressed by his audience. He knew the men from the crew, and they hailed him with a mixture of respect and laughter.

Greasy Galt beckoned to Matt. "Son, I want you to wheel this barrow around behind me."

"Say, Greasy, you goin' to find us another good well?" a voice from the crowd called.

"Or will this be like the one over to Gas City that struck sulphur water?"

Windy John spoke up. "If he finds oil in this cornfield, I'll spread my Stetson with axle grease and eat it for bread and butter."

"Well, now, Windy John Boston, old friend, if you feel that way, there must be some reason," one of the men exclaimed. Matt recognized him as the tool pusher for the Company.

"I'm willing to bet on Greasy," someone else shouted.

"Windy John knows more about doodlebugging than Greasy will ever know. Five dollars says there ain't no oil in this cornfield."

The men began a wild scramble to place their bets on the well.

Pa raised his voice, "There will be no gambling on my oil well!"—but it was lost in the shouting.

Greasy left his tinkering to step into the group that was making bets. "Just a minute, you fellows. I say I will get ten percent of the take on this little game or I will pack up my marbles and go home. Right?"

The derrick crew agreed.

"Just to show you," continued Greasy, "what faith I have in my Oil Detecto, I promise that if Detecto does not tell the truth, I will push it into the Verdigris River."

Cries of approval echoed from the crowd, which was growing steadily. Matt wished he had something he could bet with, but that would have been a sin in Pa's eyes. He was impressed with Greasy's confidence, but most of all, he wanted an oil well to be someplace in that cornfield. Perhaps if he had faith that a well was down there, there would be one. Would believing make something come true? Was this a case of faith or superstition? It took millions of years to produce an oil pool. His willingness to bet money on it wouldn't magically bring a well into existence. This was logic, but he still wanted to bet on it.

Greasy Galt picked up the copper-tipped branches that sprouted from the machine in his wheelbarrow and started walking. He and Matt went zigzagging around in a crazy pattern, the crowd at their heels. Finally Greasy motioned for him to stop in a little hollow.

"Here it is. My Detecto says he smells oil around here and this is the spot to drill."

The bettors had been arguing with each other, and some were now exchanging insults.

Pa pushed his way into the group. "I tell you, you can't gamble with my oil well."

The tool pusher took Pa by the elbow and guided him to the edge of the group. "Now, Mr. Rempel, I'm afraid there is not much you can do about this. It isn't your well, you know. You leased it to the Company."

There wasn't a thing Pa could do, but he had registered his complaint.

The next day the crew started building the derrick. The seismologist chose a spot near the hollow that Greasy Galt had designated. Or was it that Greasy had chosen a spot that the Company had decided on? The next week the machinery was brought in and installed for doing the actual drilling for the "black gold." This was a cable drill with a bit that rose and fell, pounding its way into the earth. The crew worked around the clock in three shifts. The tool pusher came around every so often to check on tools and supplies; and the seismologist, Mr. Capley, was a regular visitor.

Matt spent all the time he could at the well, and one day the foreman even gave him a job cleaning up around the place. He earned a dollar for his work. Waldo also got a job with the crew off and on.

Mama was the one who profited most. Her reputation as a cook had reached the crew, and six of the men asked her if she would be willing to feed them a good dinner at noon. They would pay her fifty cents a meal. She was glad to do it, and she outdid herself in cooking for them. When they paid her eighteen dollars at the end of the week, she was quite overwhelmed.

"Ach, I can't take all that money just for cooking," she protested.

"You are a good cook, Mrs. Rempel. It was worth every penny."

When the construction crew moved on and the drilling crew moved in, two of those men ate their dinners at Mama's table off and on, and the family eyed her growing hoard of fifty-cent pieces with considerable respect. She put it in a luster pitcher on top of the cabinet and would not say what she planned to spend it on.

The day they spudded in, the whole family gathered to watch. John Paul was interested in the six-inch hole that was being pushed down into the center of the earth.

"Will they get to China?" he asked.

"Not even halfway," Matt answered.

"Then it is just an ordinary hole, isn't it?" With that, he lost interest.

The family settled down to the routine of the activity, knowing that it would probably be several months before they would know if they were to be oil rich or Depression poor.

One evening while trying to skip rope and set the table at the same time, Vonnie dropped a stack of plates, breaking two and cracking four.

"Oh, Vonnie!" Mama groaned.

"Nobody's perfect," Vonnie said brightly.

"Just try to be less imperfect, could you?" Mama implored.

"I'll buy you a whole set when the oil well comes in," Vonnie promised.

"When the oil well comes in" was an expression heard often, even from Pa, who warned the younger ones that there was no guarantee that the oil well would come in with oil. They might end with a water well, he cautioned.

Mama invited Windy John and Charlie over for supper occasionally. Windy John took real enjoyment in her German cooking, and in return he supplied the family with tales of his roughnecking adventures in Texas. After supper, while Matt, Charlie, and Waldo played Flinch or Rook, they would listen to tales of oil wells and doodlebugging.

"I heard of one in the East," he related. "Name of Job Moses, who got help from his Spiritualist wife. She had the spirits from the other world tell her where to drill for oil. And then there was a fellow who located a well with a ball of wax on a string. In the wax he had put hairs of a rabbit that had been killed in a cemetery during the dark of the moon. He would walk over the field, carrying his ball of wax at arm's length, and when it started swinging, he knew where to dig his hole."

"Tell us about Spindletop," Vonnie would venture from her place on the couch where she was playing with a cat called Brenda.

"Spindletop. That was a real field. They had to go down only one thousand feet and they hit a salt plug. The first six wells were producing more in one day than all the rest of the world put together."

"What's a salt plug?" John Paul asked.

"Well, sometimes salt, deep underground, is forced upward to form a salt dome, and it traps the oil. They put down so many wells at Spindletop that the field looked like a forest of wells. Oil dropped to three cents a barrel, while a cup of boiled drinking water sold for five cents. All the water around there had oil in it."

"Do you know any more doodlebug stories?" John Paul asked.

"Did I ever tell you about Zeke Proctor? He lived in a town south of here, a bachelor, seventh son of a seventh son. He was one of those who could locate water wells with a peach twig, but he felt he could use his talents for more worthwhile things, so he took up gold huntin'. Maybe your pa remembers that after the bank panics of the 1890's some of the Indians decided that a sandbank was safer than a savings bank, and they buried their gold in creek banks, and then they forgot where they had buried it. Zeke looked for this buried treasure.

"Some of the town boys thought they would play a prank on him. They planted some gold near his shack and then dug it up and laughed at him because he couldn't find gold that was right under his nose. He shook his peach branch at them; he was real mad.

"Then one night them boys dressed up in sheets and scared him when he was diggin' in a sandbank. He ran off, scared to death, and he let it out that he had been scared off by the ghosts of Indians who had their treasure buried where he was diggin'.

"Everybody laughed at him until he dug in that hole again and found gold. For a while after that, you couldn't hardly find a peach twig in those parts."

Windy John stopped talking and reached for another handful of popcorn.

"Is that all the story?" Vonnie asked.

"Almost. Zeke moved to Tulsy and bought some fancy clothes and a new buggy. He got bit by the oil bug, and he was sixty percent successful with his peach branch. Died a millionaire."

Matt said to Pa, "He sure does know the stories, doesn't he?"

Pa answered in a low voice not intended for the ears of the storyteller, "I always thought the neighbors called him Windy John because he never had anything to say. Now that I know him better, I'd say that is a good name for him."

Mama tried to shoo the little ones to bed then, but they wanted to stay up to hear more stories.

They moved fast enough, though, with a word from Pa. "I know of better uses for a peach switch than finding oil wells," he threatened.

13
The Long, Dull Winter

Nothing much happened that winter as far as Matt was concerned. The novelty of having a drilling crew on the place wore off. Roosevelt was making plans for the country, but he wouldn't take office until March. There was nothing to do but wait for prosperity. Matt looked forward to March. Somehow he had the feeling that prosperity and oil would gush forth about the same time.

In the meantime money was scarcer than ever. Pa said he sure felt lucky to have four children working, even if the four of them together didn't make more than eighty dollars a month. Mama refused to let him take Mary's wages, insisting that Mary needed them herself.

One Sunday when Mary was home, Matt asked about that money. "Mary, what are you saving your wages for?"

She had been laughing with Vonnie as they did the dishes, but now she grew sober. "I wish I knew for sure."

Vonnie had an answer. "Mary is saving for her hope chest. The bottom drawer of her bureau has sheets and pillowcases and—"

Mary clamped a soapy hand over Vonnie's mouth.

"Shh. It's a secret. And anyway, it is a hopeless chest."

Matt had never given much thought to hope chests, but he knew what they were. "You mean you are saving to get married? Who would marry you?"

Mary twisted her dishrag hard and wiped off the oilcloth table cover. "That's a good question. Who do you think would have me?"

"Well, people say Bill Jantz likes you."

"Then why doesn't he write to me? Two little postcards I have had since he went to California four months ago."

Matt watched her fling the dishwater out the back door onto the frozen ground. She wiped out the pan and hung it on a nail under the sink and spread the dishrag and towel neatly on a string back of the stove.

Matt asked, "Does he write to anyone else? I mean, do any other girls get letters from him?"

Mary turned to look at Matt. "No. I'm sure he doesn't write to anyone else. Not even to his mother. Now that's something to think about, isn't it? I am the only girl he has sent a postcard to." She smiled. "Thanks for the happy thought, little brother. Now what can I do for you? Any problems you want solved?"

Matt wasn't sure why his question had changed her mood, but he was glad to have her gay again.

The weather turned very cold in the middle of December, but they were prepared for it. Already in September they had moved the cookstove from the summer kitchen into the house.

One of the chores of winter was to see that there was fuel for the stoves. There was a vein of coal back in a pasture about a foot underground, and Waldo and Matt worked at uncovering it, prying it out of its bed with pick and shovel, and getting it stored in the shed back of the kitchen. This was hard, dull work, and Waldo kept trying to think of ways of making it easier. He could come up with nothing in the way of an improvement. When the boys asked their father for a change of work, he assigned them to sawing blackjack, the tough scrub oak that grew along the creek, but that was just as bad.

When fired up with coal or blackjack, the cookstove could throw out a lot of heat. When the weather got really cold, however, they had to bring the tall base burner into the front room. It was five feet high and had a domed top with a fancy nickel-plated curlicue on top. The door had isinglass windows that let the fire shine through, and there was a nickel-plated rim around it about knee high. They pulled their chairs up to it and tilted back with their feet on the shiny skirt. The base burner drew the family around it like a hen with chicks, and they stood near the stove even though they were too warm there.

The bedroom was unheated except by the stovepipe. The pipe went from the stove through a hole in the front room wall, into the bedroom closet, out into the bedroom. Then it turned sharply as a hairpin and went back into the closet and back again into the living room to connect with the chimney on the other side of the room. No heat was wasted.

Christmas came that Depression year of 1932. Even though the country was still singing "Happy Days Are Here Again," they had little cause for singing if they counted only their material blessings. But Matt sang *"Stille Nacht, Heilige Nacht"* at the Christmas Eve program at church with his class. He felt that he had a reason to sing.

John Paul had a piece to speak at the Christmas program and he hated it. Only his mother's gentle persuasion got him to appear in front of those people to recite the poem that Vonnie had written.

Christmas joy's in all the land
We give to you a welcoming hand.
This program we've prepared for you
Because we want you happy too.

They rode home in the wagon under cold starlight. Waldo had not been able to start the car all that day, so they had bundled into the wagon, burrowing in the straw to find the hot soapstones and covering themselves with horseblankets. They were not uncomfortable. Matt, tucked between Mary and Menno, sang "Joy to the World" with them in English. The words and the music expressed exactly what he felt, and he was grateful that somebody had written it for this occasion.

When they got home, Pa added more coal to the kitchen fire, and they sat around the table eating the treats they had received from the Sunday school. To the hard candy and peanuts, Pa added what he said was to be their Christmas present from him, an orange for everyone. Mama set a dish of *Pfeffernuesse* (peppernuts) on the table. Matt had helped his mother make the tiny spicy cookies this year and he appreciated them more than he ever had before. He had thought he would go crazy cutting the dough into quarter-inch cubes.

The one kerosene lamp in the middle of the table gave a warm glow to the kitchen, and to Matt everyone in the family seemed golden and beautiful.

The surprises came the next morning. Then they opened the box from the grandparents in Kansas. There was a shirt for every man and boy, a dress for Vonnie, and handmade sheets for Mama and the older girls. Grandpa had also included candy and nuts. Everyone agreed that there were many families worse off than the Rempels were that Christmas of 1932.

But Christmas was not yet over. Mary and Esther brought in their present for Mama, an enormous box that had to be carried in by Lester and Menno. It was a rug, a red plush, flower-bordered, white-fringed rug, and it made her cry. The family gathered around her to wipe her tears and point out how beautiful it was and to assure her that of course she deserved it. Nothing was too good for their own mother. They pushed the furniture back and laid the rug in the middle of the front room. It was so beautiful that the boys were afraid to walk on it with their everyday shoes.

The next surprise was a gift from Waldo. He had fixed up the lamp that Matt had won so that Mama could put a kerosene lamp on the base, and the flame would glow through the parchment shade to illuminate the roses. Everybody admitted that the rug and the lamp gave the whole room an air of elegance.

The last surprise was for Mary. The Voths had gone to California to visit their married daughter. They stopped Mary in church on Christmas morning to give her greetings from Bill, which she passed on to the family at the dinner table.

"Did they say why he doesn't write?" Menno asked.

"Mrs. Voth said that Bill is working two shifts a day at

MERRY CHRISTMAS
FOR: MOM

the creamery. One of the men quit and Bill took his job along with his own. When he has a day off, he just sleeps. But he told Mrs. Voth he would be back in June and that I should be ready for him."

"What does he mean, be ready for him?" Waldo asked.

Mary shrugged. "I wouldn't know. But he sent me a present." She showed them the little pin made of seashells that Bill had sent along with Mrs. Voth.

"Two shifts a day!" Lester exclaimed. "That's what I call being buried in his work."

John Paul looked thoughtful. "Didn't you say he makes ice cream and cottage cheese? What do you mean, 'buried in his work'?"

Mary turned to Les. "You said it. You explain it."

For Christmas dinner the Rempels feasted on a traditional menu. Mama had saved back a ham for which she had made fresh horseradish sauce. There were fried potatoes, rye bread and *Zwiebach,* and for dessert *Pluma Moos.* The *Moos* was made of dried fruits thickened with plenty of cream. Who could think of a Depression when there was such food?

But Christmas was soon over, and life settled back to its routine of nothing happening. The older ones went back to their jobs; Vonnie and John Paul went back to school after an extended vacation, for the school board was scrimping on the teacher's salary by shortening the weeks of school.

When the weather was good, Pa kept Waldo and Matt at the everlasting job of picking coal. Waldo also had a few traps on Crooked Creek that he and Charlie tended, but trapping didn't amount to much because the animals had moved out to deeper streams with much higher water.

The daytime work was sometimes hard for Waldo and Matt, but Ma usually fixed an early supper, and the winter evenings were long. Often they would go to the neighbors for talk and guitar music and Flinch or Rook. The Berg boys came over at least once a week, and Charlie oftener than that. Sometimes all of them sang verse after verse to Karl's guitar and Charlie's harmonica.

One evening after Charlie had gone home, the Rempels and Bergs still sat chewing over the "old maids" in the popcorn bowl.

"I hear that Charlie is an ex-convict. Is that so?" Karl asked.

Waldo said noncommittally, "Who told you?"

"Tim Steiner heard it from a friend of his, the deputy sheriff."

"If Tim knows it, everybody knows it." Waldo spat a hard kernel into the woodbox. "Does he seem like the criminal kind?"

Karl said, "He seems like a real pleasant boy."

"Very obliging," Cornie added, drawing on his four-buckles, getting ready to leave. "He offered to help me with skinning skunks, if I ever trap any."

"He's the most obliging fellow in the world," Matt said knowingly. "I figure that is why he got into trouble. He's always ready to help somebody."

"And his Kansas City friends took advantage of him. Of course, that doesn't excuse him," Waldo said defensively, "but when you know how he lived on the streets without a good family, it is easier to understand why he got into trouble."

The Bergs left, and Matt went to his cold sheets feeling a little sorry for Charlie since Tim Steiner knew about his past.

They butchered in February, and that was a high point for Matt. Butchering, in fact, was the most interesting event of the year, except for threshing. Here again, several neighbors exchanged help, but this time the women came with the men.

They had fresh liver for dinner, although Matt didn't care much for it. He did like the spareribs. They tossed the fat from the hogs into the big black kettle outside and melted it down. When it was sizzling, they threw in the fresh spareribs to fry. Crisp hot ribs, eaten in the cold, were a once-a-year treat.

Butchering offered another advantage. Mama could now make soap from the fat. Washing dishes without soap had been a greasy, messy chore. However, at about this time Pa decided that they must sell all the cream and not make butter, so they were reduced to lard for their bread. The Depression was not over.

The weather turned blustery the last half of February, as if to give one parting blast before spring. Pa didn't press the boys to do anything but the chores. Matt had wonderful hours for reading, but he soon ran out of material. He had reread his school books until he knew them by heart. Finally, in desperation he went back to the box of books under the bed, those his father had brought home from the sale last fall. From the tattered, unattractive volumes he chose *Gulliver's Travels.*

Matt told Cornie about the book one Sunday afternoon as they were at the kitchen table playing checkers.

"There were these Big Endians and Little Endians and they had a big fight over which end of the egg you should break, the little end or the big end."

"That sure sounds silly," Cornie commented as he crowned his king.

"Do you know what those Big Endians and Little Endians remind me of?" Matt asked. "They make me think of the different churches, fussing about how they should be baptized and whether they should wear buttons or hooks and eyes, or one suspender or two suspenders."

Cornie was shocked. "But these are important matters! Of course, it is silly to argue about which end of the egg you break, but I don't think you should compare that with rules that might help you get to heaven."

"But if I want to wear two suspenders, you have no right to insist that I wear only one," Matt persisted.

"What's got into you! I have never tried to tell you how many suspenders to wear."

"I need a crown for my king," Matt said and dropped the subject.

Gulliver kept Matt entertained through February, and then he heard that Mr. Capley thought they would know in a week or so what kind of well Rempel No. 1 was going to be.

Things were going to start happening.

14
Rempel No. 1 Comes In

No one could miss the fact that it was March and spring had arrived. The snow melted just in time for the chick-weed to appear, green and lacy in the yard, and when the hens were let out of the henhouse, they scratched for it with a springtime carol of clucks.

It was still cold at night, of course. The snow that had melted off the roofs by day became long icicle swords by night.

Roosevelt took office and began immediately to do something about the Depression. One of his first maneuvers was to close the banks for three days. They opened after the bank holiday on a sounder basis. Everyone knew that things would be better. The federal government was taking an interest now, and people would never again lose money that they had put in the bank, either because of robbery or the bank's failure.

During the winter, the Rempel family had been able to agree on one subject. They all, except Mama, wanted to go to the Chicago World's Fair.

In Chicago exciting things were going on. The World's

Fair was to be held on a man-made projection of land in Lake Michigan. "A Century of Progress" was the theme, and it was to be "a gesture of faith in the future," as Matt read about it, and "a repudiation of fear and depression." Fantastic buildings, prehistoric animals, futuristic transportation were to be a part of the "Rainbow City." Matt yearned to see it, and Pa promised that if the oil well amounted to anything they would celebrate by going to the World's Fair for an "educational experience."

Mama said, "I'll stay home and milk the cows."

The work on the oil well continued now at a steadier pace, and Matt spent some time each day watching them drill. As they bored deeper into the earth, closer and closer to the oil that they all hoped would be there, the tension and excitement increased. Even the men who had bet that there wasn't any oil hoped that there would be. Greasy Galt came out every day, and at least once a day he would get his wheelbarrow off his truck and test again, each day reaffirming his original opinion. There would be oil in that hole, he declared.

Windy John came over every day, and his supporters would ask him if his peach twig said the same thing, and each day he repeated his opinion. There would be no oil in that hole.

It was hard for Matt to keep his mind on the daily work when there was that oil well over there in the cornfield. Matt could hardly live with the suspense. He felt excited and jubilant. And he felt lucky. Unknown to Pa, he took the three dollars he had earned and gave it to the tool pusher for a bet on Rempel No. 1. If you feel lucky, shouldn't you trust your luck?

Then one day the drill was down to the depth at which the geologist had expected to hit oil, and still there was no sign of a pool. Greasy Galt said cheerfully, "Just keep going, keep going. It's just a little deeper than I had reckoned on."

They kept going for two more days, and then the foreman reported that they could expect action soon.

Action was what they got. At midafternoon Matt heard the rumble of the expected explosion deep inside the earth. He thought how lucky he was that he would be there to see his well come in. The explosion ripped up through the hole, sending rocks and mud into the air. The men rushed to control the showers, and Matt crawled under the back of Greasy Galt's truck and watched from there. It was a scene of frantic activity, and Matt felt elated that something finally had happened.

The explosion didn't amount to much, he decided, for the men soon had the well capped and were examining the debris that had erupted.

And then Matt realized that something was missing.

Rocks and mud and water had come flying out of the well, but there had been no oil in that eruption. All he could think of at the moment was that he had lost his three dollars. He crawled out from under the truck and went to join his father, who was talking to the foreman.

"It looks as though we hit a gas vein, Mr. Rempel. There is no sign of oil."

"Doesn't the gas mean that there is oil down there?" Pa asked.

"It could mean that. There are few oil fields without gas, but there are gas fields with no oil. There may be a gas cap on top of the pool of oil if there is more gas than the oil can absorb. On the other hand, it may be that there was an oil pool here and that oil has now turned to gas."

Later that day, after the men had drilled farther and tested and conferred, Mr. Capley said, "I'm sorry, Mr. Rempel. It looks as though there isn't anything here. That was a little natural gas vein we hit and it doesn't even amount to much."

"You don't think there would be oil farther down?" Pa asked.

"No. I think we would be wasting our time to do any more drilling. We have hit shale. This is not oil well gas. I'm going to tell the men to pull the pipes and we will move on. We'll put a cap on this to keep it from catching fire. Sorry, Mr. Rempel. That's the way the oil business goes."

"We are sorry we are not millionaires, but it is like Mama says, God never promised us an oil well. It is too bad that the Company lost all that money putting the hole in."

Mr. Capley shrugged. "It wasn't a total loss. We learned some things about the earth's structure around here. The more we know, the less of a wildcat operation this becomes. There is bound to be oil around here, and we'll find it as soon as we know enough."

Mr. Capley turned to direct the men to start pulling out.

Matt had forgotten about Greasy Galt. He looked around for him and saw his truck hightailing it out of the field.

"He's going to dump his Detecto in the Verdigris, no doubt," laughed one of the crew.

Matt walked back to the house by himself, sick with

disappointment. He felt as nauseated as if he had eaten something that didn't agree with him. The oil well had been his highest hope, and he had believed in it more than he should have. But telling himself that he had been foolish did not make him feel any better about it.

There was no hope for anything now. He was stuck. He had no room left for dreaming.

He went into the barn and sank into a pile of hay.

He had prayed. Should he keep praying? He had prayed for the oil well, he had prayed for the refrigerator, and he had prayed for anything that would make it possible for him to go back to school. Was this then his answer to prayer? No more school? God wants you here on this farm, helping your parents. Your father is right, schooling isn't for good Mennonite boys. It will corrupt them. You must stay home if you are to be a good Christian.

God's will. He had heard that phrase ever since he could remember. He thought of his mother using the phrase when she spoke of the death of a baby, a girl who had died when Matt was two. Bow to God's will, she said. How could you be sure some things were God's will? A baby's death? The hunger of the people that he saw along the railroad track in Tansy? Farmers like his father losing their land? How could God will such things for his children?

Spud crept along the dusty floor of the driveway. He crowded into Matt's lap and licked his hand. Spud—that symbol of all things ordinary, familiar, and unexciting. Matt patted him and stroked his back, getting some comfort from Spud's concern. He felt like a Spud; they had lots in common.

It was time to start feeding the horses, milking the cows,

tending the chickens. Was there no end to it? He felt an almost physical pain at the thought of getting up and doing the chores. But he could hear his father and Waldo coming into the barn, so he grabbed a pitchfork and started tossing hay into the mangers.

Supper that night was a quiet meal, with Vonnie and John Paul doing most of the talking. Mama tried to cheer them up, but she was not the joking kind.

"We can't miss what we never had. I hadn't learned how to run that new washing machine, anyway," she said brightly.

Suddenly Vonnie started to cry. "Now I can't buy Mama the dishes to pay for the ones I broke," she wailed, and ran into the bedroom.

John Paul was glad to find a use for his good word again. "Alas, alas. We are not rich. Shall I sing you a song?"

Without permission, he launched into a song that he had learned at school.

> Grasshopper sitting on a carpet tack,
> Sing Polly wolly doodle all the day.
> A-pickin' his teeth with a railroad track,
> Sing Polly wolly doodle all the day.

The family forgot about their lack of wealth for a few minutes while they tried to convince him that he had the words turned around.

"A grasshopper wouldn't pick his teeth with a railroad track. That would be silly," insisted Vonnie, who had returned to the table.

"Well, it's a silly song. It is supposed to be funny."

Vonnie said, "I know a joke about picking teeth. Do you all want to hear it?"

"Tell us," Mama encouraged, while Matt and Waldo groaned at the prospect.

"There was a henpecked husband looking in the window of a dentist's office at all the sets of false teeth that were for sale. 'That's a good-looking set,' the man said. But his wife said, 'Henry, how many times have I told you not to pick your teeth in public?' "

"You have been reading my *Literary Digest*s," Matt growled.

Waldo said quickly, to ward off any more jokes, "Mama, I have been thinking. Maybe we can fix something up for you out of this oil well yet. Maybe I can surprise you."

Although everyone wanted him to tell them then and there what the surprise would be, Waldo would not say another word about it.

He did some very mysterious things for the next few days. He started digging a trench that began at the abandoned oil well and ran along the fencerows toward the house. Matt watched him until Waldo made him grab a shovel and help.

"What's all this for?" Matt asked.

"I won't tell you until it's ready. You might not like the idea. Just keep digging toward the house."

It was a long way from the cornfield to the house, and Matt grumbled all the way. It took the two of them three days, using their spare time, to complete the trench, and the only reason Matt kept at the job was that he wanted to find out what Waldo had in mind.

Then Waldo asked Pa, "That money I made working with the oil crew—it's mine to spend the way I want to, isn't it?"

Pa looked at him warily. "Depends. You thinking of spending it on foolishness?"

"I'm thinking of spending it for Mama."

Pa hesitated a moment more. "Yah, you can spend it."

Waldo took his money from the dresser drawer, got into the car, and disappeared for the afternoon.

When he returned toward chore time, Matt surmised that Waldo had been to his favorite place of recreation, the dump. He had all kinds of odds and ends of scrap metal and valves and things Matt didn't recognize as anything.

"This cost money?" Pa demanded as he surveyed the pile of trash.

"No, this didn't cost anything. The Company is going to deliver what I spent the money for."

The next day a truck stopped to dump a load of one-inch pipe in the barnyard. Matt helped Waldo distribute the pipe from the oil well to the yard.

"What kind of harebrained scheme is this?" he demanded. "You know as well as I do that there isn't any oil in that well, not even enough to wet this little pipe."

Waldo worked far into the night for several nights on his pile of trash, and when it got to the place that he thought it was shaping up into something, he banned the family from the summer kitchen and wouldn't let anyone see what he was doing. He spent every minute that Pa would spare him on Saturday morning. Then he insisted that all of the family go to town that afternoon. He would have the surprise ready when they got back, but they were not to hurry.

While in town Matt learned some startling news that made him forget about Waldo and his contraptions. The crew that had been digging at Ben Voth's had struck oil. It was estimated that Voth No. 1 would be a big producer. That gas light at the Voths' swimming quarry had been the clue to an oil well. He also learned that Tolliver No. 2 had come in.

Ben Voth! The most prosperous member of the Zion Mennonite Church. What kind of justice was that?

On the way home, Matt protested to his parents, "Why should Ben Voth strike oil when lots of people who need it more than he does don't get a drop? He already has all the money he needs. And why should the Tollivers have two wells?"

"The rain falls on the just and on the unjust," Mama quoted. "I suppose you could say the same for oil wells."

"Ben Voth would be one of the just," Pa corrected. "But you can say that oil wells have a very hit-or-miss way of coming in."

When they got home, they found a grinning Waldo at the kitchen table. He didn't say anything. Vonnie rushed from room to room asking, "Where's the surprise?" Matt couldn't see anything in the kitchen, but when he went into the front room, he noticed it right away.

The old base burner had been transformed. Through the isinglass window you could see the flickering flames of a fire that burned with no visible fuel. The bucket of coal had been removed, and the box for wood that had stood behind the stove was gone.

They all stood speechless around the new stove.

"Mama," Waldo said proudly, "you are the only housewife in the Zion Mennonite Church with clean, dustless, odorless, gas heat. You now own a gas-burning coal stove.

John Paul had to have explained what was burning. They all offered Waldo their congratulations and thanks, but then Waldo had one more surprise. He touched a match to the lamp on the table and presto! Matt's prize lamp blazed forth with a light that made the roses glow thirty times brighter than they had with kerosene light.

Waldo's project had been to bring gas into the house for a stove and light. He had succeeded.

"No more coal pickin' for us," he nodded to Matt.

Pa reminded them that they would still need coal for the kitchen stove, but that didn't seem like such a chore.

Mama drew up the rocking chair to the gas stove and sat down. "I have the finest parlor in the state of Oklahoma with my red carpet, my fine stove, and my pretty lamp. It will be nice when the folks come to visit, isn't that so, Papa?"

Pa drew his chair up and put his feet on the fender. "Yah, they will think we are doing well."

"Ach, Peter, we don't need to put on airs with them. The stove and light will make them more comfortable."

"I don't want to show off," Pa defended himself. "I just want your pa to think you married a good provider."

"Peter, I don't complain to you or to the Lord about the way you provide. I know I married a good man and so does my father. As I said, the stove and lamp will make them more comfortable when they come to visit. Maybe I am too proud about the rug. It is so pretty."

Matt took his *Good Housekeeping* and sat down to read under the bright lamp. It was good that his family could feel so happy about the lamp and the stove. Matt would have preferred a gunny sack full of money.

15
The Tragedy of Weather

The warm weather of May continued into the middle of March, but everyone knew that it couldn't last. So when Charlie came over one soft sunny day to ask if Waldo and Matt could go fishing, Pa said, "You boys know that the barns need cleaning and Mama is after you to get the hen house disinfected. We ought to get the place raked up before Grandpa Enns comes. But go ahead."

They drove over to the Verdigris and anchored their poles in the bank. They lay around on the new grass talking about weather, oil, church, and baseball. Almost reluctantly they tended their lines when a catfish came up to snap at the bait.

"Fishin' has never been better," Waldo observed. "Let's get these cleaned and start a fire."

"Did you ever stop to wonder how so many fish get in these little rivers?" Charlie asked. "And even in ponds that don't have outlets?"

"I always thought they swam up from bigger rivers," Matt said, although he had never thought about it before.

"Uncle John says it's ducks."

"Ducks!" Waldo stood up after starting his fire. "I never heard that ducks bring fish up river."

"They bring the eggs on their feathers as they stop off at one place and another on their way north."

"Ain't that the berries!" Waldo exclaimed. "I never knew that."

Charlie nodded. "Uncle John knows all kinds of things like that. I hope I live long enough to learn everything he knows about oil wells and animals, and farmin'."

"You could go to school," Matt suggested.

"Nope. First I will learn all I can from him and then I would like a little farm of my own."

Waldo glanced at the river. "Hey, you two, you both have bites. Are you here for fishin' or talkin'?"

Two days later a north wind brought in a fresh bit of weather that even Oklahoma saw very seldom. There was a hard rain, a drop in temperature, and a sudden freeze. The world was glazed with a treacherous, beautiful coat of ice, and the temperature stayed at ten degrees above zero for four days. Cattle struggled and slipped to get to the frozen-over water tanks; men walked cautiously and complained of muscle-ache at night because they had held themselves tense all day while working about a frozen farmyard. The country school closed because the children could not get there. And everybody went ice skating on the hay meadow.

The ice storm caused an accident at the Boston farm.

Pa owed Windy John a day's work, so Windy John asked if Matt could help him cut corn shocks out of the ice to feed as fodder to his cattle. The three of them—Windy John, Charlie, and Matt—chopped away at the shocks with their broad-bladed corn knives. It was hard work, for there was such a glaze of ice on the ground that Matt spent half the time picking himself up.

The accident happened while Matt had his back turned to the other two. He was working at another shock when he heard a yell from Charlie. Matt turned to see Windy John sprawling on the ice, his corn knife flung from him. Charlie was leaning over him, his knife in his hand; and Matt saw that Charlie's knife was covered with the blood that was flowing from a gash in Windy John's forehead.

Matt was paralyzed. His first thought was that Charlie had attacked Windy John and killed him. Matt felt like taking off for home as fast as he could fly over the ice, and perhaps he could save his own head. Charlie was a thief and a killer, and he would now want to kill Matt because he had witnessed his crime.

But there was Windy John—to leave him lying there bleeding to death was impossible. Matt realized that he must somehow move his weak legs, overcome his nausea, and quiet his trembling hands. He threw down his corn knife and stumbled across the ice to Windy John.

"What happened?" Matt asked, kneeling at the side of the old man.

"I—I don't know. I slipped. I mean he slipped. My knife—" Charlie seemed too frightened to make sense. Matt forgot his fear of Charlie as the two boys tried to stop the flow of blood with their handkerchiefs.

They asked each other if they should try to move him to the house or run for help. Matt was prodigiously grateful when a neighbor, Tim Steiner, stopped along the road and asked if he could help.

They loaded Windy John into the back seat of Tim's car, and Tim and Charlie took off for the hospital at the county seat.

It all happened so fast that just four minutes after he heard Charlie yell, Matt found himself alone in the cornfield, with only the discarded corn knives and the blood on the ice as evidence of the accident. Matt decided that now he could go home. He skated and skidded over the rough ground as fast as he could go. His family was astonished when he told them about the accident, but he did not say anything about his first fears of Charlie.

Tim Steiner came by later, very upset. "I want to know how that accident happened," he demanded of the assembled Rempels, who had never got back to work since Matt had reported the accident. "I thought maybe Matt would know. This Charlie is a graduate from reform school, they tell me, and I have my suspicions. Matt, you were a brave boy to face up to Charlie. I think he was trying to kill Windy John."

Matt answered uncertainly, "Charlie didn't try to kill Windy John. They were working together and Charlie's knife slipped. It was icy, you know."

"Did you see it happen?"

"No," Matt admitted. "I was about thirty feet away at another shock of corn. But I don't think Charlie would try to kill anybody."

Waldo said, "Charlie is trying hard to live a good life and he thinks a lot of Windy John."

It was obvious that Tim Steiner was not satisfied with this doubtful defense. "I want to hear what Windy John has to say when he comes to."

"Now, Tim, give the boy a chance," Pa urged. "Don't say anything until you do hear Windy John's side of it."

Tim Steiner left muttering, "Once a crook, always a crook."

Pa was so disturbed by his neighbor's visit that he decided to go see Windy John. "We don't want that kind of talk around the neighborhood," he told Mama. "I'm going to the hospital, and I want Matt to come with me."

It was a slow and slippery drive to the county seat, and it was noon by the time they arrived at the hospital. There was no one at the front desk, nor was there anyone in the long dark hall that stretched before them.

"I'll just look around a little," Pa said and started sauntering down the hall. He stopped at a door near the end, looked in, and motioned to Matt. Matt hurried after him, and they entered the small room to find Windy John sitting on the edge of the bed, fully clothed, including a head bandage, trying to tie his shoe.

"I am sure glad to see you," he said in a loud whisper. "Shh, don't let the nurse hear you. She's off eating her dinner, and I'm getting out of here. No need for me to be here, anyway. I don't know why that Tim Steiner had to bring me clear over here when Doc could have sewed me up in his office. Come on, Matt, see if you can tie my shoe. I get dizzy when I lean down. Now where are you parked? Out in front? Help me into my sheepskin."

Pa protested in a loud whisper, but he couldn't change Windy John's mind. "If you don't take me home, I'll walk. Go on, do as I say. I don't hold with hospitals."

So Matt and Pa slipped out as quietly as they had come in, and Windy John tried to keep his metal-tipped leg from making a racket as he tiptoed down that corridor. They made it safely and tucked Windy John in the back seat of the car and drove off.

"Now tell us what happened to you," Pa demanded when they got out of town.

Windy John was half reclining in the back seat, holding his bandaged head, and Matt wondered if he was regretting his hasty exit, wishing he were back in bed under the soothing hand of the nurse.

"Man, am I glad to get out of there. That was a battle-ax of a nurse. She wanted me to eat something she called bull-yon. I told her I was a vegetarian, but she spoon-fed it to me. Imagine a grown man like me bein' fed with a spoon."

"Forget about the hospital and tell me what happened," Pa insisted.

Windy John lost his sputter. "I don't exactly know. I slipped on the ice. This blasted tin can on my peg skidded and I fell. After that, I don't know what happened."

"Charlie hit you with his corn knife. By accident," Matt said quickly.

Windy John closed his eyes. "I was afraid that's what happened." He sat without speaking for a mile or so, and then he said, "I don't want nobody to hold it against Charlie. I know it was an accident."

The Tansy community was not so sure. Word of the mishap got around in a hurry and everybody had his own ideas about it. People discussed it in the stores and mulled it over in the churches. The more they talked, the more they became convinced that the "accident" was no accident. Charlie had without doubt tried to kill Windy John so that he could have his farm. They didn't have a logical explanation for why Charlie would want to do such a thing or how he would think he could get away with it. They repeated Tim Steiner's phrase: "Once a crook, always a crook."

An ugly fear settled over the community. There was a dangerous ex-convict in their midst, and they shunned him.

About a week after the accident, Matt went to town with Waldo on Saturday night. Just before they were ready to start home, Waldo gave Matt a nickel and told him to go buy a bottle of pop for the two of them while he loaded the groceries and the empty egg cases.

Matt was standing at the soda fountain with some of the town boys when they started talking about Charlie.

"Maybe we should run him out of the country on a rail," one of the boys suggested. "An ex-con and a killer, that's what he is."

"That's what we ought to do. We don't want him around here."

Matt listened openmouthed. They were talking about an easygoing, friendly boy who had never caused them any harm. Matt felt that he should speak up. What they were saying was not true. He looked around for Waldo, but he wasn't in sight. How could Matt speak out to these boys with whom he hoped someday to go to school? Did he dare disagree with them?

"Let's go over there some night and beat him up. All of us together could catch him in the dark and show him how we feel. How about it, Matt? We could meet at your house."

"You can't do that!"

They all turned to look at Matt. "Why can't we?" the biggest boy asked.

"Maybe here is another one we should beat up. Are you a friend of Charlie Boston? Why can't we beat him up?" One of the boys grabbed Matt by the shirt collar.

"Charlie is just as decent as any of you. He had some bad luck, but he isn't mean or tough like you guys," Matt exclaimed.

There was a roar of rage from several of the boys, and one of them came at Matt with his fist drawn. Matt wished desperately that Waldo would come in.

"Take back what you just said," the boy ordered. "Take it back or I'll cram my fist down your throat."

Matt looked into eyes dark with anger. The fist under his nose looked powerful enough to knock him cold. "Charlie Boston is not mean or tough or a killer," Matt quavered, scared almost speechless, wondering if he would come out of this experience alive.

He watched unmoving as the other boy drew back his fist for the punch. Matt waited for the wallop. Then four loud thumps sounded on the wooden floor of the store. The boys dropped back. Matt looked up to see who his savior was, and he saw Windy John in the doorway. Windy John motioned for Matt to come, and he held the door open for him as he went out.

Matt leaned against the front of the store, weak with relief.

"Thanks, Matt, for sticking up for Charlie. That took nerve, and I appreciate it."

"I was so scared I could hardly talk," Matt confessed.

"Being scared has nothing to do with having courage.

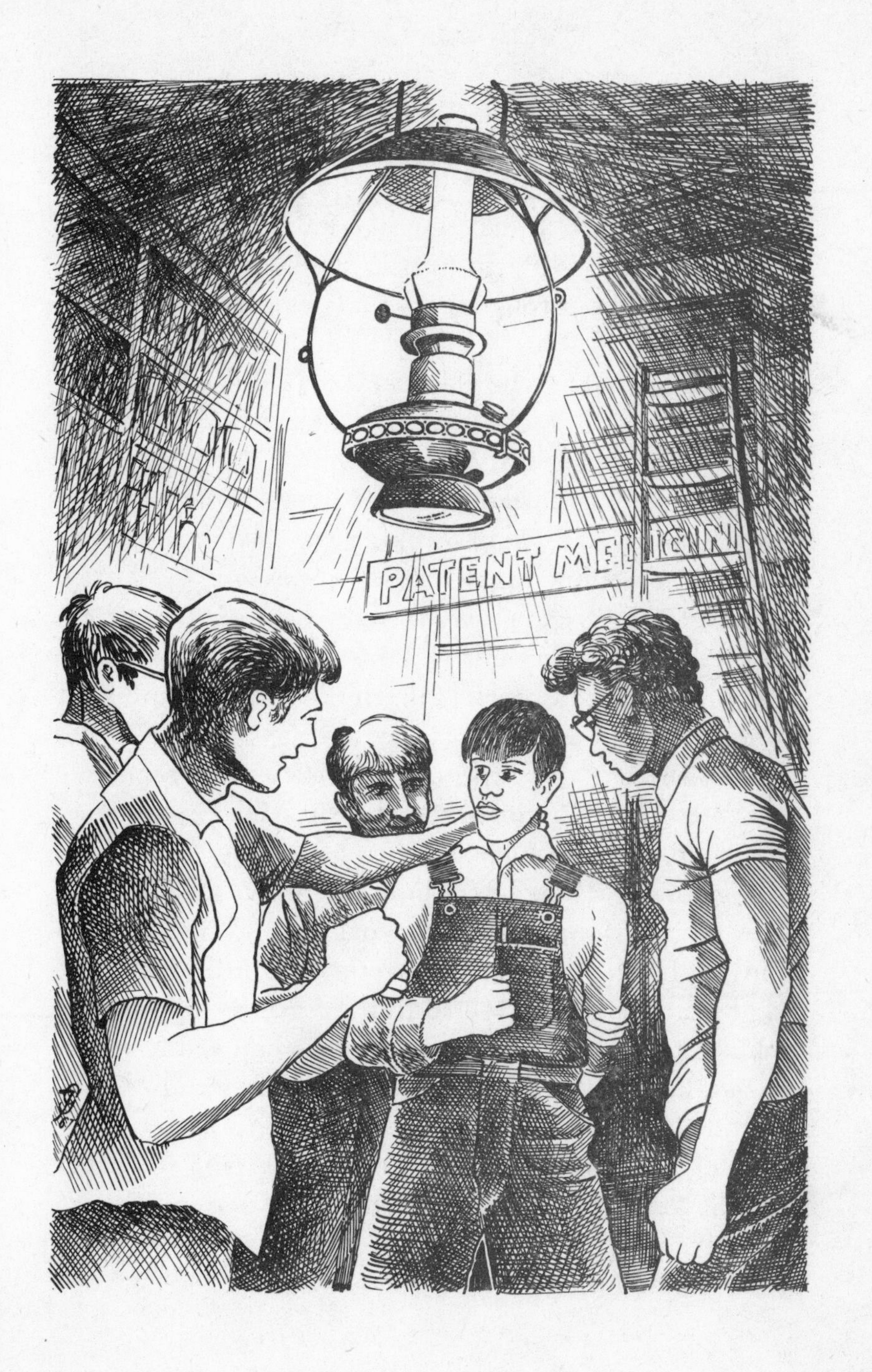
PATENT ME

I admit you surprised me. I kind of had you down in my books as someone who would turn and run. You are a lot like your pa."

"Like Pa! I don't think I am like Pa at all."

"Yes, you are. Now go find Waldo and get on home before one of them roughnecks finds you out here in the dark."

Matt trembled all the way home. He was glad he had done what he did, but he couldn't help wondering what would have happened if Windy John had not come along. One thing he was sure of. He had lived through the experience. Maybe it would be easier the next time that he had to do something impossible.

Stormy March gave way to balmy April. On a fresh and pleasant Monday morning just three weeks after the ice storm, Matt was busy gathering the dirty clothes for washing in the backyard. He would have known it was April by reading the papers. There were daily reports of tornadoes, sometimes in Arkansas or in Missouri, or closer to home in southern Oklahoma.

He started the long job of pumping water for the wash. Here he was, doing woman's work again. He wouldn't mind washing clothes if nobody ever found out, for he didn't really find the job so dull. Washing might be a backbreaking job for a woman, but he enjoyed using his muscles, lifting, stretching, pushing. In nice weather, such as today, he could do it outside, heating the water in the big black kettle over an open fire and dipping the water from the kettle to the washer. He added the shavings of strong lye soap that his mother had made when they butchered, and then he put the clothes in the washer.

This was an automatic washer, but it was not like the ones he had seen advertised in *Good Housekeeping.* As he pushed a lever, the clothes in the washer automatically swished around and got clean. Matt considered his machine one step above the washboard, which he still used for the very dirty clothes. After he had worked on a load long enough, he put the clothes through the wringer. This was automatic, too. As Matt turned the handle and cranked the wet clothes through the rubber rollers, the clothes automatically became somewhat dryer.

"I should have been called Kilowatt, the way I supply power around here," he thought. "I'll have to tell that joke to Vonnie."

He was hanging the overalls on the fence just before noon when he noticed that the warm spring sun had disappeared. He looked up to see clouds boiling in from the west. They looked a lot like those clouds that had brought the wind and rain last August when Windy John had lost his buildings.

Waldo came in from the cornfield where he had been plowing. He was covered with dust, and so was Pa when he came in from planting oats.

Pa looked at the rolling clouds. "Maybe they will bring a good rain."

They washed up for dinner and went inside while Matt finished hanging up his wash. He kept watching the sky. One of the clouds was clearly separating itself from the rest. While Matt watched, it formed into a funnel with the narrow end appearing close to the horizon. It looked like the twisting smoke of a locomotive.

Matt knew what a funnel meant: tornado! He rushed

to the front door to call to the family, "A tornado's coming!"

There was a scraping of chairs; his parents and Waldo rushed out on the front porch to watch the tornado, which was approaching now very rapidly.

"I wish we had a storm cellar," Pa exclaimed, as he always did before every storm that Matt could remember. "Let's all get into the corner of the front room where we will be safest. Anyway, it ought to miss the schoolhouse by a good mile." That meant that Vonnie and John Paul were safe enough.

The four of them sat silently in the northwest corner of the room on Vonnie's bed. Spud crawled under it, but he was the only one small enough to squeeze under. Mama sat holding her luster pitcher of oil money and Pa sat with his arm around Mama. Matt and Waldo kept going back and forth between the cot and the window, not minding Pa's demands that they get away from there and keep out of the way of shattering glass. Not that the glass was shattering, but that Pa expected it to explode at any minute.

"Hey, my wash is flying all over the place," Matt shouted.

"What are a few rags?" Pa exclaimed. "Get over here."

Matt felt very excited, but not afraid. Nobody he knew had ever been hurt in a tornado. Somehow tornadoes had always skipped over the Rempel farm in past years.

Then Matt saw the tail of the cloud race toward the house. He thought at first that it was headed directly for their corner. Suddenly it seemed to turn to take a more southerly path, and finally they saw it blow across the farm just south of the buildings. He saw the hens run toward the coops, their feathers blown up over their heads. Then the next moment the feathers were smoothed down in the opposite direction. Matt could not be sure which way the wind was from when it went by. It seemed to be from all directions at once, and the sound was that of a furious storm.

There was a small shower, a few spattering drops. The Rempels went out into the yard to feel them, stretching their hands out, but hardly getting wet. They watched as the tornado went southeast toward Windy John's cornfield.

On the Rempel farm it seemed that nothing was seriously hurt: the hens looked healthy, the horses were safe in the barn, and the mules were kicking up their heels in the lot. There was not even a broken window. All the damage had been in the form of flying boards and trash which were scattered around.

"Let's get this cleaned up before Grandpa and Grandma come next week," Mama said.

After dinner Waldo went back to his plowing and Matt to his washing. He hunted all over the farmyard to find the clothes, and he found everything but Pa's nightshirt, the one that said "Fast Rising" across the chest. Mary had said when she made it that it was an appropriate message, and Pa had always been a little proud of it. Matt started pumping water and heating it all over again for the half-day ordeal.

Pa was just ready to hitch the horses to the wagon so he could go sow the last of the oats when Waldo came galloping in on one of the mules.

"Old Kicker got hit by a wood fencepost down in the

pasture. It went right through her hindquarters and is still sticking there. Bring a gun so we can put her out of her misery."

"Himmel!" Pa exclaimed, using the strongest word in his vocabulary. "She was a good milker, too. We can butcher her, maybe, and save some of the meat. Matthew, run down and see if somebody from Bergs and Schmidts can help us butcher this afternoon. I'll give them each a quarter. It won't keep very long. We'll need that hot water for the butchering."

So Matt had to put aside his washing to help with the butchering. The neighbors came over and they made fast work of it. Mama took an optimistic view of the butchering. "She was the hardest cow we had to milk, so if one of them had to go, God chose well. And this way we will have fresh meat when Grandma and Grandpa come next week."

After a late supper of fresh beef, Pa, Waldo, and Matt sat around the kitchen table helping Mama cut up beef for canning. There was a knock on the back door, and Karl Berg came in.

"Did you forget something?" Pa greeted him.

Karl shook his head slowly. "No. I come with bad news. Charlie Boston was hurt bad by the tornado. They took him to the county hospital, but he died this evening at six o'clock. I thought you folks would want to know. Windy John is taking this pretty hard."

"But the tornado didn't touch Windy John's place. It went between our two farms. How could it be?" Waldo expressed all their unbelief.

"That's just it. If Charlie had been in at dinner where

he was supposed to be, he wouldn't have been touched. He was out trying to finish up the plowing. Windy John went out to warn him about the tornado, but while they were still in the field, the tornado came right at them."

"But Charlie can't be dead. Are you sure? I saw him just yesterday." Matt wanted to argue, to deny, to make the words not true, but Karl merely shook his head.

Pa asked, "Was Windy John hurt?"

"No, and the reason he wasn't was that Charlie saved his life. Windy John says Charlie pushed him down in the furrow and lay on top of him. Charlie was killed by a flying post."

Charlie had died a hero.

They sat in stunned silence for a moment, and then Mama wiped her eyes with her apron. Matt felt that it was more than he could take in. Such things were not possible; was this what the preacher meant by someone's being taken "in the twinkling of an eye"?

After Karl left, Pa put on his hat and went to see Windy John. The rest of them went back to the task of preparing meat. Nobody had much to say except now and then to remember something about Charlie, how nice he had been or that they knew he had reformed and would never have been in trouble again, and how lonely Windy John would be now.

Matt thought about Charlie for a long time before he went to sleep. How could God do this? On what basis did he decide who would live and who would die? Was there an answer?

Two days after the tornado, they all went to the funeral at the Zion Church. They joined their silent neighbors who came to shake Windy John's hand and wish him well. Some of them even said they were sorry that they had misjudged Charlie, for it was now clear to everybody that Charlie had never tried to kill Windy John. The Tansy community recognized that Charlie Boston had been a brave man.

Mama brought Windy John home for supper after the funeral and then sent him on with a loaf of fresh bread and a pie. This was the best way she knew to ease pain, and Matt wished he could do something like that.

He thought a lot about Charlie during the next few days. As he helped clean up the debris, as he did the washing over on the next bright day, he had time to think.

Charlie had had courage. He had been willing to give his life for what he believed in, and he believed in Windy John. He had not turned tail and run like a Spuddy dog but had deliberately laid down his life and said, "If anyone is going to be hurt here, I will be that one."

Matt remembered now the words of the preacher at the funeral, words that he hadn't thought much about when he heard them: "Greater love hath no man than this, that a man lay down his life for his friends."

"That's the kind of courage I believe in," Matt told himself.

16
Grandpa Enns Expresses an Opinion

A letter came from Grandpa Enns with the definite news of their promised visit. They would be coming back with the Voths when they visited Kansas the middle of April.

The family was sitting at breakfast when John Paul asked, "Is Grandpa's last name Kansas?"

"His last name is Enns and he lives in Kansas," Mama said as she set his oatmeal before him.

"Is he old?"

"Well, he is about seventy-five. I hope you little ones won't make fun of his beard."

"Oh, Mama. We know better than that," Vonnie protested.

"And don't stare at him when he puts sugar on his eggs," she said, removing the sugar bowl from John Paul's reach before he could add a fourth spoonful to his oatmeal.

"Sugar on his eggs!" All the children, even Waldo, were shocked.

Later as Matt pushed and pulled at the lever that turned the dasher to make the clothes slosh in the washer, he thought of the coming visit. Maybe Grandpa would buy Mama a washing machine. Matt might even put in a few words about how big a job it was to do the washing for a family of eight children. He wouldn't mention that four of them were not home, and he wouldn't mention that the job of washing was his own responsibility.

He had heard a good deal about how Grandpa did not believe in playing favorites among his children. What he did for one he tried to do for all. Grandpa had had nine children. He had given each of them eighty acres of land.

Could Grandpa be persuaded to pay Matt's way through high school? Probably not. He would want to do the same for all his grandchildren. But perhaps none of his other grandchildren wanted to go to high school. Maybe he could be convinced that Matt was a special case.

The clothes were clean by then, and Matt started putting them through the wringer. Pa stopped on his way to the barn. He seemed to have something on his mind and didn't know just how to say it.

"Matthew, I wonder what we should say to Grandpa Enns about how you want to go to high school. I don't know how he feels about schooling. He might not hold with it."

"But shouldn't we tell him?" Matt asked, dismayed.

"Well, yes, we have to tell him. But remember that if Grandpa Enns doesn't go along with it, you can't go, even if we have the money."

Pa jammed his hat down over his head and went on to the barn. Matt started cranking the wringer again, wishing his father didn't put so much store by what Grandpa thought.

Matt thought one rinsing was good enough for getting the soap out, but Mama made him rinse twice. That meant that he had to pump more water. He used the rinse water to pour on the new garden and the soapy water to wash off the porches. Everything had to be clean enough to eat on before the grandparents came.

He wondered if his mother expected Grandma to look into her dresser drawers or go out to the hen house to see if it was clean. Was Grandpa going to notice that they had swept the cobwebs out of the summer kitchen, a building they would not even use for another month?

The only way you could explain his parents' concern was that the grandparents must be hard to please. They were old people. Matt knew about old people. There were a number of them in the church, and they thought that young people with young ideas were sinful.

Grandpa and Grandma would be like that, disapproving of what young people liked to do. Back in his mind Matt had a thought that he would not put into words. It had to do with God's way of doing things. If he wanted to take a soul to heaven, why had he chosen Charlie rather than an older person? Not his grandfather or grandmother, for that would have distressed his mother, but some cantankerous old man who had lived his life? Grandpa would think that questions like that were wrong.

Just a few days before the expected visit, Mama instructed Pa to buy some new dishes when he went to town. "We have so few uncracked plates that I'm ashamed to set the table. Just find some plain white dishes at Edwards." Mama took some money out of the hoard she had saved from boarding the oil crew.

When Pa came home, he had a real surprise for her. He had found some tin dishes at a good bargain and had bought a whole set of eight plates, cups, saucers, and cereal dishes. They were white enamel with a blue edge.

Mama looked at them with dismay. "But for company, Peter! For us for every day, yes, but for my father and mother who have a set of Bavarian china?" And then she realized that she had said the wrong thing and turned to put them away. "They were a real bargain. We will use them. Dishes are not really important."

Matt saw her wipe her eyes on her apron when she went to the stove to put a fork in the potatoes, but he also noiced a look of bewilderment on his father's face. It said, "I think I've done something wrong here, but I'm not sure what."

The table was set for supper with the white and blue tin dishes, and Matt thought they looked nice. He did notice that the knives and forks clattered against them as an accompaniment to the conversation.

The grandparents came driving in with the Voths one day toward evening, just in time for supper. They were to stay a week, and then the Schmidts, who planned to go to Kansas for the wedding of a granddaughter, would take them back.

Grandpa Enns was just as lively as Matt remembered him from three years ago. Mama had always spoken of him as if he were a saint, but he was just vain enough to take pride in his luxuriant beard and to deplore his scanty white hair. Grandma was still her hovering, mother-hen self, anxious to see that Grandpa was not too tired, that he ate properly, that he got the respect due him. She was a tiny woman, even smaller than Mama, but she had enough self-assurance for a woman twice her size, Matt decided.

Mama had fixed them a bed in the boys' room, and the boys had moved out into the barn for the week. The weather was pleasant, and they did not mind.

"Don't eat any of the hay," Grandpa cautioned John Paul. "Your Pa tells me you hardly have enough left for the horses."

John Paul looked at him for a moment and then said, "I don't care for hay. I will eat only the oats."

"Don't tease the children, Andrew," Grandma commanded. "They don't understand your jokes."

"John Paul and Matthew understand my jokes," Grandpa said with a wink at Matt, and Matt felt himself grow an inch in wisdom and understanding.

At breakfast the next morning Matt, Vonnie, and John Paul sat in a row across from Grandpa. Vonnie poked Matt. "Now watch him," she whispered. "See if he eats sugar on his eggs."

Mama brought a plate with two eggs, perfectly fried, their soft yolks pale in their white centers. She placed the plate before her father. Grandma, who sat at his side, reached for the sugar bowl and placed it before him. Sure enough, Grandpa took a spoonful of sugar and sprinkled it generously over his eggs. Then he ate them with Mama's home-baked bread and fresh coffee.

The children watched with mouths open. When he was halfway through the meal, he looked up at Vonnie and said, "Why do you watch me? Am I so strange?"

"It's the sugar on your eggs."

"I like sugar on my eggs. I can't think of anything that can't be improved by sugar. When you get to be my age, John Paul, you can have sugar on your eggs if you want to."

John Paul asked, "Grandpa, how long have you been putting sugar on your eggs?"

"John Paul, you are a very smart little boy. I think I will hire you to polish my gold pieces."

John Paul was not to be put off. "But Grandpa, how long have you been putting sugar on your eggs?"

"Ever since my mother made me eat them. Isn't there any subject to talk about besides eggs?"

It was nice having the grandparents around. Grandma helped with the dishes and the ironing. She was quick as a kitten and enjoyed showing that she could work as hard as someone half her age. Grandpa wasn't of much help, but he poked around the farm, looking at this and that and giving advice, which Pa took very respectfully, for it was usually good advice. In the afternoon he sat dozing in the chair on the porch.

Grandma sewed during the afternoon. She had brought lots of flour sacks with her, and she and Mama made up a year's supply of pillowcases, sheets, underwear, and nightshirts in the week she was there.

Vonnie and John Paul were still in school, so Matt had Grandpa to himself every afternoon after the old man woke from his nap.

"Do you like to read?" Grandpa asked unexpectedly one afternoon. Matt had thought he was still asleep.

Matt closed his old copy of *Literature for High Schools* and sighed. "I wish I could find more books."

"You planning to be a preacher? You need to read a lot to be a good preacher. I have lots of books in Kansas. I could have brought you some, but I didn't know I had a grandson who liked to read."

"I don't even know if I would like to be a preacher. I wish I could go to school and find out what I would like to be. I might even want to be a farmer, but first I would like to go to school."

"Now, that's a question I wanted to ask. Why aren't you in school?"

Matt told his grandfather all about his problems. He told about how there was not enough money to send him to school and hire someone to do his work now or when Waldo would leave home. He told about his disappointments of the oil well and the contest.

"You say you won that beautiful lamp in your front room? That's quite an accomplishment."

So Matt went on to tell him even about the silly idea he had had of winning the reward money and how he had turned in the wrong man. Grandpa listened with such good attention that Matt looked up once to see if he had gone back to sleep; but he was listening, bright-eyed, his elbow on the arm of the rocker and his chin on his fist, so you couldn't tell from the shape of his mouth how he felt.

"Should I ask him if he has any money to help me through high school?" Matt asked himself.

Grandpa folded his hands across his stomach and started to rock. "Son, you know I gave each of my children eighty acres of land. I gave all the land away except the eighty we live on in Kansas. I don't have any extra money, and if I did, I couldn't help just one of my grandchildren when I have forty-seven of them.

"But I want you to know," he continued, "that I think you should go to high school if you can manage it. I believe education is important. All of my children in Kansas are trying to give their children a high school education. Some of the grandchildren are even going to college! You have to be prepared for what God calls you to do, you know."

"Could you tell that to Pa?" Matt asked.

"Yes, I'll tell your pa that, if it will make any difference," Grandpa promised.

At that moment they saw Beauty coming down the road, and with the arrival of the children their conversation was at an end. Matt felt better than he had in weeks. If Grandpa approved of his ideas, they must not be sinful.

All the Rempel children came home on Sunday to become reacquainted with their grandparents. Lester also brought Gloria so that Grandpa could meet her. The grandparents exclaimed over how the children had grown, and the children exclaimed over the fact that the grandparents did not look a day older than they had three years ago.

But Grandpa reminded them, "Even if there is snow on the roof, that doesn't mean that the fire is out."

Later in the afternoon when all the family was out in the kitchen except Matt and Menno, Grandpa Enns came to sit beside Menno.

"Tell me," he asked, "have you picked out a nice girl yet?"

Menno said lightly, "Oh, I like all the nice girls." But

then his tone changed. "No, I don't. I like one especially, Ruth Yoder."

Matt could not help exclaiming, "Nancy John's oldest girl?"

Menno said firmly, "That's the girl. I suppose I would have to join her church because if she joined mine, she would be banned from their society. I couldn't ask that of her. Of course, I can't get married for a couple of years yet because Pa needs my wages."

Grandpa nodded. Matt went into the bedroom and almost giggled. He was glad that Menno had found himself a nice girl, but it seemed kind of a joke on Menno and maybe a bit of a joke on Pa, for he surely had not expected his lighthearted son to fall in love with an Amish girl.

After the older ones had gone back to their jobs that evening, the rest of the family sat around the small gas fire in the front room talking about them. Pa expressed his disappointment that all but Mary seemed to be finding wives and husbands outside the Zion church.

"Are they not good young people? Would they do better by marrying in their own church?" Grandpa asked.

"Oh, these are fine young ones. Now you take the boy Esther goes with, he's a good worker and very decent. I can't think of a thing wrong with him. But he is not one of ours."

Grandpa Enns pulled on his beard thoughtfully. "I have always believed that the Mennonites are only a part of the kingdom of God, perhaps included in the family to safeguard certain ideas that the other brethren might overlook."

"Now, Grandpa," Matt willed silently, "say something about letting me go to high school. Tell Pa it's all right."

But the conversation turned to other subjects.

Monday was a warm, balmy day. Matt was out spading the garden, turning the earth over for a planting of sweet corn.

A fat worm slid off his spadeful of dirt.

"Here, put it in this tin can," a voice behind him said, and Grandpa stooped down to crumble the clods in search of more worms. "I wondered if your pa would care if we went fishing, and he said we should take the buggy and go over to the Verdigris, just you and me. Do you want to?"

"Sure, let's dig our worms and get going."

Grandma packed them a lunch, and they rode away in the buggy with the mended shaft that Waldo had wired together.

Grandpa was good company, and Matt got him started telling of the pioneer days when he had come over from Russia to settle on the Kansas prairie.

"We brought over silkworms and planted mulberry trees for a silk industry, but that never amounted to much. It took too much time that we needed for farming. And we brought over Turkey red wheat seed. I was about your age at the time, but I remember my brothers and sisters picking over that wheat a kernel at a time to select the finest seeds we had. We did well with that wheat, and now most everybody in Kansas plants wheat bred from that strain."

"Why did you pick Kansas? It seems to me there must be prettier parts of the United States to settle in."

"The Santa Fe Railroad was anxious to have settlers. We had to choose between Nebraska and Kansas, and

Kansas looked the more promising. Those early farmers had their problems, but they prospered."

"Wasn't it dangerous?"

"It was living. Living is dangerous. We had weather and sickness. We had people getting hurt by falling off barn roofs. Some of them died of that killer, old age."

They had reached the bridge over the Verdigris River, so they tied the horse to a cottonwood tree and walked downstream.

"I don't know about the fishing here, but this looks like a good place to sit," Grandpa said, and he sat down on a log with his back against a tree.

Matt put a worm on his hook and threw it into the river, and then he sat with his back to the log.

"This is pretty fine. I don't get a chance to go fishing very often. Your grandma won't allow it."

Matt turned to smile at the old man, and he caught a twinkle from his eyes. Matt decided that Grandpa understood Grandma pretty well.

"Your ma tells me you joined the church last fall. Was that an experience like Paul's or more like Thomas's?"

"It wasn't any Damascus road experience. What about Thomas's?"

"Oh, you remember that Thomas had to have everything spelled out for him before he could accept Christ."

Matt thought about this as he watched the cork bobbing gently in the ripples. "I suppose it was more like Thomas's. I never was sure that I was ready to join—'born again' like the preacher said. When the Sunday school teacher asked us if we didn't want to go forward, I just went along with the rest, but I had all kinds of questions in my mind that didn't seem to bother anybody else." Matt had never spoken of this to anyone before.

"Don't you feel that you want to be a Christian and a church member?"

"Sure, I do. I think you have to live according to the commandments and the way Christ taught if life is to make any sense."

Grandpa reached for one of Grandma's sandwiches. "Like the preacher said, there is this matter of being born again. You have to make your start somewhere, and that is what you did. You are making your start. Now you have to grow, and you don't do this all in a day."

"But I have so many strange feelings about God," Matt confessed. "I know all the things we learned in Sunday school about God, how good he is and how he loves us. But look at what has happened to our family just in the last few years. And here this year we lost the lease money, and the well didn't come in. Was that because God didn't want us to have money? And then the tornado killed a boy like Charlie for no reason at all. It makes life seem too uncertain."

Matt's voice took on a note of self-pity and resentment. "It seems that God doesn't care a bit about me, whether I live or die or whether I go to school or not."

"You sound like Job," Grandpa said. "So many troubles, all you need is a pimple on your nose. But I'm not making fun of you. I doubt if there is a person who hasn't asked the same question you ask, and no one has a good, satisfying answer to the question of why people suffer."

"Do you mean there isn't an answer?"

"Oh, there is an answer, but I don't understand it, Matt.

Preachers are supposed to quote Scripture, so I will," Grandpa continued. "Christ says, 'I have the keys of death and Hades.' Which means, I think, that God is master over death as well as life."

This was a new idea, and Matt put it in the back of his mind to think over.

They did not catch a single fish, and they knew that the afternoon was gone by the chill in the air.

"Maybe we should get back to the house for supper. Grandma will scold me good if I catch cold in my joints," Grandpa said.

They drove back quietly through the afternoon sunshine. The cottonwood trees were just beginning to push out their leaves.

"How many seeds do you think a cottonwood tree has?" Grandpa asked unexpectedly.

"Oh, maybe a million. Sure are a lot of them in late May when they come down like snow."

"Did you ever count the seeds in a little old tomato?"

"Nope, never did."

Grandpa chuckled. "I did once. There were sixty-eight seeds in the one I counted."

"What does that signify, Grandpa?"

"I'm not sure. You think about it and see if you get any ideas."

That was the end of talk with Grandpa Enns. By seven o'clock the next morning, breakfast eaten and suitcase packed, they were sitting in the front room waiting for their ride back to Kansas.

Conversation lagged, as if everything had been said and now they did not know how to fill these last minutes of the visit. Matt wished he could think of something to say that would make his grandfather remember him as his intelligent, serious-minded, alert grandson.

Grandpa turned to Pa. "We want to get back to Kansas in time for a concert at the college. Our grandson, Henry Schmidt, is singing in the choir."

"Do you think this is good, that our Mennonite young people should go to college?" Pa asked cautiously.

"Oh, we Mennonites have to think more about education. We always need preachers and teachers. And if all of us have large families, they can't all inherit a farm, or even buy one. No, our young people will have to be trained to do other kinds of work."

"Doesn't that go against our fathers' teaching?" Pa asked, careful not to disagree.

"We Mennonites have always believed in education. The church leaders who came over from Russia had the idea of starting a seminary."

"They did?" Matt was as surprised as his father. He had always thought the elders all frowned on education.

"It is hard to convince the farm people that education is important. So many feel that all there is to life is to be born, farm, raise a family, and die right on the same farm, never knowing what is going on in the world. But there is much to learn and there are many ways of serving God."

Pa looked at Matt but spoke to his father-in-law. "If this Depression gets better, or if I could scrape together enough money to hire a man, I will let Matt go to high school. Right now I can't afford to. But I have always thought that he was a smart boy."

Grandpa looked at Matt as though he were trying to

see into his head. He nodded, "Yes, I'm sure Matt will make a scholar."

Matt began to feel like a piece of furniture whose value was being discussed, but he was relieved that Grandpa had made himself clear about high school.

A horn honked outside, and the grandparents hurried to make their good-byes.

A week after his grandparents had returned home, Matt was surprised to receive a package in the mail. It was a book, *The Mennonites,* by a man named Smith. The large, scholarly volume would have dismayed him if he had been required to read it. But his grandfather recommended it, and he had nothing else to read.

This was the story of the Mennonites as they fled from country to country looking for religious freedom, how they had become a scattered people, and why there were so many different groups of them. It reminded Matt of the long search of the Israelites for the Promised Land.

The Mennonites had been persecuted in Switzerland, hounded in Prussia, betrayed in Russia. Many had come by various routes and at various times to America, feeling always that they were being guided by the hand of God.

What a long line of ancestors he, Matthew Rempel, had to look back to. And now he was a part of the line, a line of people who down through the ages had made up the Kingdom of God. His descendants would become part of the line.

"But don't I have to be alive to help form the line?" he thought, remembering Charlie Boston.

Charlie should not have died. But because he had died, everyone in the community had been a little strengthened by his act of unselfishness. Some people make the line strong by dying, Matt decided.

Matt put his book aside in the hay and looked up into the rafters of the barn roof. It was quiet enough to think about things that Sunday afternoon in late April. He thought about his ancestors and the Kingdom of God; about Charlie and living and dying; about what Grandpa had said about making a start someplace. Then he was glad that he had joined the church. Not all of his questions had been answered, by any means; but now he felt sure that he wanted to be a part of the Kingdom of God.

17
Mary's Wedding

On a Sunday in May after a family dinner, Mary announced her news. "Bill and I are getting married in June—I think."

Esther jumped up to run around the table to hug her sister and the boys congratulated her. Evidently she had already told her parents, for Matt thought they nodded with approval but not surprise.

Matt said, "What do you mean, you *think* you are getting married?"

Menno said, "She means if Bill can get the day off."

Vonnie said, "She means if *she* can get the day off."

Lester said, "Or does she mean if Bill can catch a ride home?"

Mary pulled an envelope from her pocket. "This is the first honest-to-goodness letter that Bill ever wrote me. It has seven lines. Let me read it. 'I am getting the month of June off and starting right out for Oklahoma. Why don't you go buy a new dress and set a date with Reverend Reimer? Any day will do as long as it is after I get there and before I leave. I would sort of like to see the Chicago

World's Fair before we settle down in California. See you, Bill.' "

There was a pause at the table, and then Menno said thoughtfully. "He doesn't say anything in there about getting married, does he? Just tells you to make a date with the preacher."

"I wonder if he plans to go to the Chicago fair by himself," Waldo said, helping himself to the last of the *Pluma Moos*. "Maybe he would rather take a bunch of the guys. I'd sure like to go."

Lester asked, half seriously, "How are you going? He hitchhiked out of here, if I remember."

"Oh, Bill will come riding out of California in his golden chariot. He will sweep Mary off her feet and gallop off down Route 66 all the way to Chicago." Menno grinned at his sister, who seemed to enjoy the teasing.

Mama broke into this bantering. "That's enough of teasing. We need to plan the wedding. What date do you think, Mary?"

They looked at the calendar. Lester figured that it would take four days to hitchhike from California if Bill was lucky. He should be here at least by Monday.

"Then let's plan the wedding for Thursday. Thursday afternoon for the wedding and Thursday evening for the reception," Mama decided.

"That will be just after harvesting. Yes, we can make it," Pa approved. "We will invite the church and the Kansas relatives and set up a tent and serve everyone in the yard."

Everyone was silent then. Matt knew they were all thinking of one thing: Weddings cost money.

Lester broke the silence. "It's a good thing Mary has worked for a year. Do you have any money saved up, Mary?"

Ma broke in before Mary could answer. "Mary will need her money for her new house." She looked at Pa.

Pa answered her look. "I will pay for Mary's wedding. And for Esther's and for Vonnie's. We won't have anything fancy, but it will be a good wedding that will last the rest of your life."

"What can you sell?" asked Waldo, the practical.

"I had thought we could sell old Kicker until she got hit by the tornado," Pa said unhappily.

"How about Hardtail?" Matt suggested.

But after considerable discussion they decided that they could not sell either of the cows.

Without saying anything, Mama went to the cupboard and got down the luster pitcher. She brought it to the table and dumped out the contents. With their doubtful help, she counted the money and announced with satisfaction, "I have forty-nine dollars and fifty cents left from feeding the oil crew. That will be a good start."

Mary came over behind her mother's chair and put her arms around her. "Mama, you are dear. That oil well was worth something. The well and Mama will pay for my wedding."

The talk turned to other details that Matt was not interested in, dresses and things that no boy would give a hoot about. Then Mary spoke to him directly.

"Mama thinks you can wear those short pants to the wedding that Waldo outgrew three years ago. Then we won't have to buy you a new pair."

"I will not wear knickers. All the boys will laugh at me. I would rather wear overalls." He had been wearing overalls to church since he had outgrown the last pair of Waldo's knickers.

"Mr. Hadley wears knickers. Every time he goes golfing." Esther tried to smooth his wounded feelings. "You will look nice in them."

"I will not wear knickers," Matt repeated.

"Put a little sugar on them," Menno advised.

The joke about sugar had become a family response to any complaint. Ever since Grandpa Enns had said he believed that anything could be improved by sugar, someone was bound to suggest sugar as a cure-all. When Menno complained that the cuff of his white shirt had been scorched, Matt would advise him to put sugar on it. Even Mama caught on. When Pa fretted because the milk tasted like wild onion, she passed him the sugar bowl.

Nobody paid any attention to Matt's revolt. They went on to talk about John Paul. They wanted him to speak a piece at the reception.

John Paul also took a strong stand. "I will not speak a silly piece in front of a lot of people."

"Oh, this will be a nice piece. Just a little welcome to let the people know that we are glad they came."

"I will write a poem for you," Vonnie promised generously.

"School is over. No more pieces," was John Paul's last word.

But nobody paid any attention to him. It was all settled. Matt would wear knickers and John Paul would speak a piece.

The wedding preparations offered a new plan to Matt for getting money. Matt could not see how he could earn money in a community where there was no money. But there was money in Tulsa. Mary would be inviting her employers, the Fowlers, to her wedding. Who had more money than Mr. Fowler? And furthermore, who was more generous than Mr. Fowler? He had recently given the money for a new wing to a large church in Tulsa. Surely he could afford a few hundred dollars for such a worthy cause as Matthew Rempel.

So he entered into the plans for the wedding with more enthusiasm than he might have otherwise. He wouldn't tell anyone of his plan. He would just carry it out by himself.

Mary quit her job and came home to stay two weeks before the wedding. Esther took her vacation during that time so she could help with the preparations. They flew into the work yet to be done. Matt had thought that the place looked clean enough for anybody, but Mary sat down at the kitchen table one morning to make a list of jobs that Matt would never have thought about.

"You must wash the windows on the outside on the day before the wedding. If there is anything certain in this uncertain world, it is that it will rain right after you wash the windows," Mary declared.

"Then why don't we wash them whenever we need rain?" John Paul asked reasonably as he passed from the front door to the back.

"You'll want the rug taken out and beaten," Esther advised, and Mary wrote that down.

"We'll ask the Voths and other church members if they

can take care of the Kansas relatives. I wish Grandpa and Grandma Enns could come, but it is too hot for them to travel. Imagine all these dozens of cousins coming from Kansas just for my wedding!" Mary exclaimed.

"The harvest season is later in Kansas and they have time on their hands right now," Matt assured her.

Esther went to wash the bedroom windows and Matt and Mary started on those in the front room. Matt was surprised to see Mary sink down on Vonnie's cot.

"What if I am just imagining that Bill wants to marry me? What if he doesn't really mean it and won't show up?"

Matt tried to reassure her. "He'll be here, don't worry. He wants to see that Chicago World's Fair."

Mary shook her head. "I'm serious. Don't tell Mama, but sometimes I get such a feeling in the pit of my stomach. I'm scared."

"Scared! What is there to be scared of?" Matt had always thought that his oldest sister was the least scarable member of the family.

"You know what a clown Bill is. Maybe he didn't mean that letter the way I took it. He never came out and said he wanted to marry me. Did he? What if he was only joking? What if he doesn't show up?"

"You know better than that. Bill wouldn't joke about marrying you. And you wouldn't want to marry him if he was only a clown."

"Matt, you are a comfort. Well, if worse comes to worst, I can always go back to my job at the Fowlers'. You know, Bill did write a card to his mother saying he was getting tired of doing his own cooking and living on pork and beans. I think he needs me."

"I'm just worried about his hitchhiking home. What if he gets here two weeks after the wedding?"

"I'm more worried about hitchhiking back. I can cook, but can I cook like a hobo?"

Her good humor restored, Mary went to help Esther with the bedroom windows.

The family kept reminding Mary that Bill would arrive on a horse to sweep her off her feet. Pa thought it probably would be a mule, but Vonnie had in mind a snow-white charger bearing a Prince who would come to awaken his Sleeping Beauty.

"Is California farther than Tulsy?" John Paul asked.

"About fifty times farther," Vonnie answered, more accurately than she realized.

"Then a horse will be mighty tired," John Paul nodded knowingly.

"Sleeping Beauty refers to Mary, not the horse, you *Glummskopp,"* Vonnie scoffed.

Finally the day came that Bill Jantz, the shining knight and bridegroom, was expected to arrive on his snow-white steed.

"Would it seem funny if I spent the day at Jantzes waiting for him?" Mary worried at midmorning. "Will he let me know when he comes or will he be so tired out from hitchhiking that he'll go right to bed? I wish we had a telephone."

Matt tried to keep an eye on the road, but it seemed to be an unusually quiet day for traffic. His job for the morning was to fill all the mattress ticks with fresh straw, and he was done by dinner time.

They had a sketchy meal of ribble soup, a thin milk

soup with a noodle mixture dropped into it. Waldo said that this was no meal for a working man, and the girls defended themselves by saying that they had more important things to do than cook. And anyway, who had an appetite?

"What is more important than keeping me from starving?" Waldo demanded.

"Sewing a lace edging on a wedding veil," Mary answered with spirit, jabbing a hairpin back into her black bun. "I have been working since before breakfast, and I even forgot to take time to comb my hair."

"Right after dinner you clean up and change into something nice," Mama commanded gently.

"Would you have a handout for a bum?" asked a voice from the doorway.

They all turned to look at the thin-faced, dusty stranger who stood there looking so sad.

Mary jumped up so fast that she knocked over her chair. She was in his arms before any of the family realized that the stranger was Bill Jantz, steedless.

"Who is this woman who throws herself at me?" Bill inquired straight-faced of the gaping Rempel family.

"Bill, I knew you would come!" Mary wept.

Mary's tears seemed to surprise Bill. He lifted her wet face from his shoulder and said, "Mary, Mary, did you doubt that I was coming?"

Mary shook her head wordlessly. The rest of the family descended on Bill before they could say more. While the handshaking took place, Mary dried her eyes.

They had all kinds of questions for him.

He tried to answer them all. "Well, like the man said,

here's the kettle of fish in a nutshell: I just this moment arrived from California. I have not been home yet and I have not had my dinner."

Esther and Mama started frying potatoes and eggs for him while the rest of the family sat around listening to his tall tales of travel.

"Did you hitchhike or ride a snow-white charger?" Vonnie asked.

"I didn't hitchhike."

"Then let us see your horse," John Paul insisted.

"Come on, I'll show you."

Bill took them to the yard to show them his new tan Chevrolet sedan. "I thought this would be more like a married man's car, sober color, solid build. It ought to last forever, and it runs twenty-two miles to the gallon."

"That's more like a chariot!" Vonnie exclaimed.

Mary approved of it. "This looks like a fine family car. I won't worry any more about hitchhiking to California."

The next few days went fast. Mama and the girls made crocks and crocks of *Zwiebach* dough which the church women took home to bake. Mary's friends were also baking the cake. The cheese, lunch meat, iced tea and coffee, and ice cream were ordered for a wedding *Faspa* for two hundred and fifty guests.

"You didn't forget to invite the Fowlers, did you?" Matt asked Mary.

"Of course not. Mr. Fowler said they would be the first to come and the last to leave. He wants to throw rice at us when we drive off."

Throwing rice didn't make sense to Matt. Nobody brought rice to Zion weddings.

OKLAHOMA
19RD64
Jan Gleysteen

The wedding was set for three o'clock at the church. One errand had been left till the last minute. Bill and Lester had to go to Tulsa to pick up the flowers. They left in Bill's car at one o'clock, and they planned to be back in time to deliver the flowers to the waiting bride and get her to the church at one minute before three.

Mary and Esther retired to the bedroom to dress. Matt changed into the hated knickers in the summer kitchen. He had given in about the knickers because he thought they might impress Mr. Fowler more than overalls. After he was dressed, he went to wait on the front porch. He noticed a darkening in the sky to the west and a let-up in the heat. Someone, somewhere was getting a nice rain.

At twenty till three Karl Berg arrived to pick up Esther, John Paul, and Vonnie. Karl joined the rest of the family on the porch. Mary and Esther appeared. Mary was pale and beautiful in her white satin and filmy veil. Esther was crisp and regal in blue dotted swiss. Even Matt thought they looked *schmuck*.

The time for departure came and went, and still there were no flowers.

"Oh, well," Vonnie said cheerfully, "you really don't need flowers for a wedding. We could go ahead."

"But I do need a bridegroom," Mary reminded her. "I'll just wait."

Matt looked at his sister's serene face. She seemed to have lost all doubt of Bill's willingness to be married. Matt was less certain. He had read some stories in *Good Housekeeping* about bridegrooms who panicked at the altar.

At that moment Matt saw a blur of car whizzing up the road. It turned into the yard and stopped with a screech.

Two mud-splashed men, one carrying a gladiola bouquet, raced for the steps.

Mary said, "You are certainly the latest thing in bridegrooms. What happened to you?"

"We got caught in a rainstorm and then got stuck in the mud on the way home. I'll be cleaned up in ten minutes."

The wedding started half an hour late, but from then on everything went perfectly. Matt was relieved to see that the Fowlers were present. He would surely have a chance to talk to Mr. Fowler at the reception.

After the service, the congregation all returned to the Rempel farm for the wedding *Faspa.* Pa had rented a tent and the guests were seated at tables and benches made of planks. Matt and Cornie ate together in a corner of the tent, although Matt could have eaten at the bride's table.

Most of the neighbors had to go home to do their chores. During that time Bill, Lester, and Matt managed to wash the mud off Bill's new car. There was a problem: Where should Bill hide the car until he and Mary were ready to leave? If they did not hide it, there would be some jokers who would unhook the ignition, smear the car with "just married" signs, and tie on tin cans and old shoes. They could not think of a good hiding place.

Matt finally came up with the winning suggestion. "We could put it under the Crooked Creek bridge. There is no water in the creek, and you can't see under the bridge from the road, and nobody will be wandering along the creek today."

The three of them drove nonchalantly out of the yard with a vague explanation to the onlookers that Bill needed something from home.

They turned at the corner and drove a quarter of a mile to the bridge. Bill drove down the gentle bank and parked the car neatly in the cool shadows under the bridge. Then the boys hiked home along the creek bottom, emerging from three different points of the woods across from the Rempels. They melted back into the crowd of relatives and friends with no questions asked.

Matt took satisfaction in the fact that the idea had been his and it was working perfectly.

Matt was surprised a little later to find that Cornie was already back from choring. "Are your folks and Karl here? You must have finished early with your milking." It was still daylight, and Matt had the idea that the twenty Berg cows were always milked after dark.

"Oh, I came ahead of them. I was so impatient that Ma told me to go ahead and walk, and I did."

Matt wished like everything that he could tell Cornie about the hidden car, but he didn't, feeling a little self-righteous about his ability to keep a secret from his best friend.

The tables had been taken from the tent and the benches put into rows for the evening reception. The bride and groom, still in their wedding clothes, took their places in chairs at the front. Lester was master of ceremonies and had charge of the program.

The first number was John Paul's recitation. He had been taught a poem that Vonnie had written for him:

We welcome you with roses
On this bright and happy day.
We wish for Bill and Mary
Health and happiness always.

Vonnie had spent hours over that poem, hoping to perfect it, but she never did find a way to make it rhyme exactly. The rest of the family had thought it beautiful and appropriate for the occasion. John Paul had insisted that he would not say it, but he had learned it under Vonnie's tutoring. He was to scatter rose petals as he said the words.

John Paul's name was called and he went up to the platform. Matt saw that he had forgotten to take his basket of rose petals.

John Paul stood straight and manly, and a murmur went through the crowd. "Isn't he sweet? Such a dear boy. He looks like an angel."

Moments later John Paul had lost his angelic status. As if Vonnie had spent no time at all on a fine poem for him, John Paul recited in a loud voice:

> 'Twas in a restaurant that they met,
> Romeo and Juliet.
> He had no cash to pay the debt,
> So Romeo'd what Juli'et.

John Paul marched off the platform, out of the tent, and into the night. The audience didn't quite know how to respond to the silly recitation. They were absolutely silent for half a minute; then there were a few titters and giggles, and finally everyone was laughing.

Vonnie grabbed the basket of roses and walked sedately up to the stage. The audience grew quiet as she stood there in her white voile, her black braids neat and her cheeks rosy. She spoke her piece, throwing the roses gracefully into the audience. When she was finished, the audience clapped loudly. That Vonnie! Matt thought. She might grow up to amount to something. She had brains and spunk. Maybe she would soon outgrow her sassiness.

The program continued. A men's quartet sang "The Bulldog on the Bank and the Bullfrog in the Pool." Menno did a reading about a fat lady at a baseball game, in falsetto voice. Finally there was a call for Bill to sing, and with a broad wink at his wife he sang their favorite, "I Wish I Was Single Again."

Matt slipped out after that to go look for John Paul. He found him in the haymow asleep.

"Come on, wake up. You want some ice cream and cake, don't you?"

John Paul stood up and brushed off the hay from his black stockings. "Is anybody mad? I said I wouldn't say that piece, so I couldn't, could I?"

"They have forgot about it by now. Come on."

When Matt went to get his ice cream, he saw a good opportunity to talk to Mr. Fowler. Mrs. Fowler was visiting with Mama, and her husband was standing a little apart. Mr. Fowler looked successful. He was lean and straight with a touch of gray in his brown hair. There was one thing that was out of character about him. Although he was neatly dressed in a dark suit and he had a diamond pin in his tie and a gold watch chain across his vest, he had calloused hands and dirty fingernails.

"Mr. Fowler, I'm Matthew Rempel. Do you remember me?"

Mr. Fowler turned to him and exclaimed, "Of course I do. How are you? Are you enjoying your sister's wedding?"

"Oh, sure."

"Let's see, how old are you? About ready for high school?"

Matt thought the conversation couldn't be going better. "Well, no. I want to go to high school, but Pa couldn't afford to send me this year."

"Well, next year maybe. Of course, I didn't get past fifth grade myself, but I never missed it. You can get a lot of education on your own, you know. I'm what you might call a self-made man. I started as a filling station attendant, you know, and worked up. Anybody in this country can do the same thing I did."

"Yes, I guess you're right."

"Just remember to work hard, and you can't help but succeed. This is a great land of opportunity." Mr. Fowler spread his hands in front of him. "These are the hands of a man who started at the bottom. I have worked for a living all my life. Of course, I was lucky, too." Mrs. Fowler called him then. "I see that Mrs. Fowler is looking for me. Come see us in Tulsa next time you come to town. Maybe I could find you a job in one of the stations when you are old enough. Say, I'll need your help later when we throw this ten pounds of rice I brought. Don't let Mary slip away without my knowing it."

Mr. Fowler went to join his beautiful wife. Matt sat down on the plank bench by himself to eat his ice cream slowly. Mr. Fowler was a fine man, but he clearly would be of no help to Matt.

Vonnie popped up at his elbow to tell him that Mary wanted him in the bedroom. Mary had changed into a blue linen dress on which she had pinned a small corsage.

"Can you slip this suitcase over to the car? Bill already has his in it. Hurry! We want to leave in a few minutes."

Matt took the suitcase and headed for the shadows.

Cornie was still in the tent, and Matt had the impulse to call him out. Surely at this late hour nobody would play any tricks. But Mary had said to hurry, so Matt hurried.

He walked down the creek in the dark, half feeling his way, half finding it by moonlight. He breathed with relief when he felt the car, for it was completely blacked out by the shadows under the bridge. He set the suitcase down. "Man, it's dark down here," he thought.

Bill and Mary soon joined him. Quickly Bill unlocked the car and put the suitcase in. He helped Mary in, thanked Matt for his help, and backed out from under the bridge. Expertly he eased the car up onto the road. The tires crushed gravel under its weight.

Then Matt saw the car by moonlight. It was the most painted-up wedding car he had ever seen. Except for the hood and front fenders which could have been seen from the driver's seat, every inch was covered with some inscription printed in white shoe polish. Mary and Bill blissfully and ignorantly rode away in a car that shouted "Just Married."

Matt laughed aloud. Then he realized that he was not laughing alone. Turning, he saw Cornie, Menno, and Karl slapping their knees and rolling on the ground.

"How did you guys know the car was here?" Matt demanded.

"I told them," Cornie confessed proudly. "I saw it when I walked through the woods on my way to the reception. But I told only Karl and Menno. They could have done a lot more dirty work."

"Yeah. We could have tied on tin cans or let the air out of the tires," Karl suggested.

"Or siphoned off the gas or taken out the motor," Menno added. "All we did was to polish it up a little."

They went back to the wedding reception to console Mr. Fowler. He was sorry to have lost the opportunity to throw rice. But Mama was pleased to have the ten-pound bag of unthrown rice that he presented to her.

"Mr. Fowler, you are a very generous man," she said gratefully.

Matt couldn't share her enthusiasm.

18
The Drawing: Matt's Last Chance

Prosperity was still around the corner. At least all the speechmakers and magazine writers said it was just around the corner. Congress passed laws about employment and set up the Civilian Conservation Corps for young boys to do forestry work. President Roosevelt asked merchants to put posters in their windows boosting the National Recovery Act. "Buy now," one slogan read. "Every dollar you spend goes through seventeen hands."

The town of Tansy tried several ideas that other towns had tried in an effort to bring prosperity to the stores. The businessmen got together to sponsor free movies to lure people to town.

"They come for the free movie, but they don't buy," Mr. Edwards complained to Pa.

"If they are like me, they don't have money to buy with," Pa told him. "I got to feed those steers so I can market them in the fall, and when I do, I will be lucky if I get enough money to pay the loan at the bank. Funny thing, when that bank went under, I lost my deposit, but I didn't lose my loan."

Early in July the Tansy merchants decided on a new promotion scheme that would beckon to prosperity. Every Saturday night they would hold a drawing. For every twenty-five-cent purchase, the customer would be given a ticket with a number on it. He would deposit the ticket in a big cage and keep the stub with its corresponding number. On Saturday night, numbers would be drawn, and the people with the lucky stubs would receive prizes of money and groceries. The prize winner had to be at the drawing to collect his prize.

The final, tremendous, dazzling prize on the last night of the drawing was to be a fine new Chevrolet two-door sedan. It sat in front of Edwards' store, roped off with crepe paper, the envy of every boy from five to ninety-five.

Matt thought that this was an exciting idea. Moreover, it might even be an answer to prayer.

During the month of July he decided that he would pray himself into high school. He would pray as unceasingly as any human could. He prayed every night before he went to bed: "God, find me a way so I can go. Maybe I could win some of the prizes in that drawing, and if you really want me to go to high school, let me win that car." The sale of a new car would be enough to put him through the first year.

Matt did not limit his praying to the nighttime. He tried to keep at it, giving a short prayer whenever he thought of it. In church he always added it to any prayer that was uttered by the minister.

Matt put himself in charge of collecting all the tickets that the family got when they bought their few groceries. He dropped the tickets into the cage and put the stubs carefully into his billfold. Pa didn't have much faith in drawings, but he agreed to see that Matt got to town on Saturday nights.

"If they are going to give something away, we might as well have it as anybody else," he reasoned.

Mama not only did not have faith in drawings, she believed that people should not try to get something for nothing.

On the Saturday night of the first drawing, Matt and Cornie went to Tansy with Karl. The boys rode in the rumble seat and the warm evening air of July blew into their faces. Karl dropped them off at Edwards', gave each of them a nickel, and told them to look for him about nine. He didn't tell them, but Matt knew that he was headed for Tulsa.

With two hours and a nickel to spend, the boys didn't need to be in any great hurry, so they wandered up and down the block of Main Street, talking to boys they knew and examining everything from tractors to tricycles. There was nothing to go to, and they would not have had the price of a ticket if there had been. Matt was content to finger the nickel in his pocket and debate with Cornie about whether to buy an ice cream cone or a bottle of pop.

"I'm getting a bottle of raspberry," Cornie decided. "I'm so thirsty I could spit cotton."

Matt chose pop, too, but not because he was thirsty. It seemed more dignified to be swigging a bottle of pop as they stood there outside the filling station than to be licking an ice cream cone.

The drawing started at eight-thirty, after most of the buying had been done. The crowd gathered earlier, and

TANSY OIL Co.
1207
GOOD MEALS
NIGHT OR DAY
CYLINDER OIL
KEROSENE
AXLE GREASE
TALLOW
AUTO TOP DYE
SEPARATOR OIL

they stood around in the vacant lot next to the bank where the drawing was to be held, admiring the car that was to be given away the last Saturday night in July.

The cage had already been pulled onto a platform. People hurried to deposit tickets at the last minute. One woman announced that she was going to hold hers to deposit at the very last, hoping that they would be lying right on top ready to be drawn.

She must have been disappointed, for the first thing Mr. Edwards did at eighty-thirty after he declared the cage closed was to stir up the tickets so that they were really in a jumble. Then standing up there on the platform, he made a little speech about how people should not only "Buy American," as the slogan said, but they should "Buy it in Tansy."

"The more tickets you have here in this little cage," he declared, "the faster prosperity will return. And the more tickets you have, the greater your chances of winning the beautiful car over there."

There were three prizes to be given away that night. The first was a ten-dollar bill; the second, five dollars; and the third, five dollars' worth of groceries.

Mr. Edwards called a little girl with long curls to come up from the crowd. He blindfolded her and had her draw a number.

"Draw my number, honey," came a chorus from the onlookers.

Cornie mimicked, "Draw my number, honey."

But Matt, without closing his eyes, prayed, "Please, Lord, put her hand on my number."

Matt did not win anything; neither did Cornie. They

did not know any of the prize winners, who were all from Tansy. The boys wondered if the drawing was rigged so that only town people could win.

"Oh, well," Matt said grandly. "I'm saving my best number for the car, anyway. That's the only one that really counts."

Mr. Edwards made another little speech saying that these numbers would be saved for the drawing of the grand prize, but that a new drawing would be held next Saturday night. "Get those new numbers in the cage and good luck to all of you next time."

The people drifted off then, getting into their cars to go home. Matt and Cornie sat on the old men's bench in front of the filling station until Karl arrived from Tulsa with Esther to take them home.

Matt went home empty-handed the next Saturday night and the next. He went to the last drawing with the feeling that he would have to win something this time. There were thirteen prizes offered throughout the month, including the car. Surely he would be lucky enough to win something. The Rempels deserved a prize, didn't they, to make up for that fizzled oil well?

Waldo and Pa decided to go to town with him that last Saturday night. They wanted to see who won the car. They all stood around in the crowd and talked to their neighbors. Matt saw Windy John on the bench in front of the filling station, so he went over to talk to him.

"Hello, Mr. Boston. Are you waiting to win the car?"

Windy John held out his hand for a shake. "Howdy there, Matt. Seems like I'd like to win that car as much as anybody, but I don't expect I will. Do you?"

"I sure would like to win it. Pa says we could sell it and hire a man so I could go to high school. We need a car, of course, but ours is still running. It just doesn't have anything like the style of these new cars."

"Henry Ford made a good car when he made that Model T."

Matt agreed. "Sometimes I'm afraid ours never will wear out."

They sat comfortably quiet, watching the people move around visiting.

Windy John broke the silence. "Did your pa really decide that you could go to high school?"

"You bet he did. Now it is only a matter of money. Only money. Pa wants Waldo to go out working as soon as he can find a job. Money sure is scarce."

"Yes, it sure is. But I'm glad to know your pa approves of your going to school. Hey, looks like they are ready to start. We better get over there to claim our prize."

They moved over to the edge of the crowd. Matt found his father and Waldo and stood with them.

The first prize of ten dollars went to a woman the Rempels did not know. The people around them exclaimed that she had won a prize the first night. Matt was again reminded of the injustice of fortune. Just like the oil well, the prize went to someone who didn't really need it.

He watched the drawing for the next prize, which went to one of the Rempels' Lutheran neighbors.

"Well, anyway we know of someone who won," Pa commented.

The last prize went to a stranger. Matt was a little relieved not to have won. He had kind of a superstitious feeling that his chance for the car might be better if he hadn't won any of the other prizes.

Excitement mounted as all the tickets from all four drawings were poured together into the cage. The new car sat there with its gleaming blue paint, and everyone in the crowd was hoping to win it.

A little boy about the age of John Paul was called up to draw the winning ticket. He was blindfolded with a great deal of ceremony. Mr. Edwards stirred up the tickets once more and asked the boy to pull one out.

Mr. Edwards read off the number very clearly with pauses between each digit. Matt started checking through his stubs, but before he was half through, a whoop went up from the other side of the crowd and a young man pushed forward to show his ticket and claim the car.

Waldo shouted, "Hey, look. It's Menno. Menno won the new car!"

Everyone gathered around Menno to congratulate him, and Matt felt just as jubilant as the rest of his family and friends.

"Do you know," Menno exclaimed, "that I bought just one little twenty-five-cent bottle of hair oil? That was the only ticket I had in that whole cage! I'm just plain lucky, I guess."

"Will you keep the car?" Waldo asked.

"If Pa says so."

They looked at Pa. "Well, I guess it is yours to do what you want to with since you won it. I know you wanted a car real bad. But what will the Nancy John Yoders think?"

Menno reddened but said frankly, "When I marry

Ruth, I will have to sell it, but that won't be for a few years yet. I can use the new car to go back and forth in. Yes, I'd like to keep it."

Matt turned away. He was glad that Menno had won the car. At least he told himself he was glad. But he, Matt, was the one who had counted on it. Why had he let himself hope like that? He was so angry with himself that tears came to his eyes. He knew he was a poor loser, and he couldn't help it.

The Rempels went home in their own Model T.

"It runs pretty good," Pa said by way of consolation to himself and his boys.

"It will run a good while yet," Waldo agreed. "I can keep it going as long as all it takes is chewing gum and bailing wire."

In the corner of the back seat, Matt made a resolution to himself. "I'm giving up. I will never try to win another contest, or enter another drawing, or hope for another oil well. But someday I am going to school, even if I'm fifty years old when I enter the freshman class. This Depression can't last forever."

The next morning in church he didn't know what to pray for. He had been praying, "Lord, send a miracle," and no miracle had been performed. Should he stop praying?

That afternoon after dinner he went back to his *Dictionary of Thoughts.* Out on the back porch away from the rest of the family he looked for something about prayer. He found a quotation to suit his situation exactly. "We often pray for God to add two and two together to make five." Was this what he had been doing? Perhaps the things he had been praying for didn't add up or make sense.

His mother came to the kitchen door. "Matt, I want you to take these leftovers to Windy John. They won't keep long in this warm weather."

Matt saw through his mother's words. She had baked more than her family would eat so that she could send Windy John the leftovers. He took the sack and headed toward his neighbor's house.

The hot July afternoon was very quiet. As far as he could see were motionless fields of corn, grain stubble, and hay meadow. He stopped to examine a patch of cotton that Windy John was cultivating this year. Some of the bolls had split, and Matt picked one. He tore it apart and examined the seeds. There must have been thirty seeds in the one boll. He looked around at the weeds in the fence rows, all hanging with seeds. He remembered the millions of seeds from the cottonwood trees and that Grandpa had said that a little tomato had sixty-eight seeds in it. God was certainly extravagant when he created plants. And then Matt thought he understood what Grandpa had been trying to say that day when they went fishing. God loves life: plant, animal, and human. Most of all, human life. He must love what he had created so miraculously in his image.

He started on his way again, passing Boston No. 1. He could hear its gentle pulsing. The earth, too, was alive. Suddenly Matt jumped into the air, clicked his heels together, and bounded toward Windy John's in a burst of speed. He felt glad to be alive. He was on top of the Ferris wheel.

Windy John was in his kitchen slicing potatoes with his

tiny silver pocketknife. He greeted Matt with pleasure.

"Thank your mother for the food. I sure do appreciate how she feeds me. What do you hear from your sister?"

"They are settled in California. She likes it there."

"I hear there are more jobs out there. Charlie used to talk about going to California."

Matt didn't know what to say about Charlie, so he didn't say anything.

Windy John continued, "You know, when I am plowin' or plantin' I have lots of time to think, and I think of all the things I would have liked to do for Charlie that I didn't do. I wonder what I should have done different."

"Mr. Boston, you did just right by Charlie. You don't have to have any regrets. And I'll bet Charlie was grateful that he could die by saving your life rather than by being pumped full of bullets at some bank robbery, which is what might have happened if you hadn't taken him in."

Windy John gave Matt a long look. "That's a real good thought. I'll keep it in mind. Speaking of Charlie reminds me. I talked to your pa the other day, and he said I could talk to you. I was wondering if you would consider a loan."

"A loan?" Matt asked, his mind still on Charlie.

"A loan to help you through high school. You wouldn't have to pay me back until after you start workin', and there wouldn't be no interest. The reason I make it a loan instead of a gift is that maybe when you are through with it, you could hand it over to Vonnie or John Paul if they have any of these fancy ideas about education."

Matt could find no words for this unexpected offer, and he hardly grasped the fact that Windy John was making it possible for him to go to high school.

"Mr. Boston, there is no reason for you to lend me money, glad as I would be for the use of it."

"I look at it this way. I have a little money, four or five hundred dollars, and I get a little from the oil well. I was goin' to use it to help Charlie get started on his own when the right time came. I can't help Charlie no more, but I got to thinkin' that I could help somebody. You are worth helping, I figure."

Matt was still a bit bewildered. "Why me? What have I done?"

"Nothin' special. I just think you're a good boy. I liked the way you stood up for Charlie when people thought he tried to kill me. I call that brave."

"Charlie was the hero—not me," Matt protested.

"I know that," Windy John said with some exasperation. "Now don't argue me down, boy. You are like your pa. You do what you know has to be done. I like the kind of person you are and I am offerin' you a loan. Will you take it?"

"Sure, I'll take it. This is what I have been praying for for a year. I just never thought I could borrow the money."

"A year ago I wouldn't have offered. I had the idea that I would get along with my neighbors best if I gave a day's work for a day's work. But you Rempels don't neighbor that way. I guess some of your ideas have rubbed off on me. Well, here we have been figurin' out how to make you an educated somebody, and I let my potatoes burn."

Matt could not remember what he said or if he said it properly, but he went home with his feet flying and his head singing.

He flew into the kitchen where his mother was wiping

the dishes. He came up behind her and threw both his arms around her waist.

"Did you know that Windy John is going to lend me the money to go to high school, and that Pa said it would be all right for me to take it?"

Mama laughed and kept on drying the skillet. "I thought that would make you happy. You see, God does answer prayer."

Matt sat down at the table. "God didn't answer my prayer. This is between Windy John and me. I prayed for an oil well and I prayed to win the car in the drawing and nothing happened. No, I can't see where God answered this prayer."

"You prayed for a way to go to school, didn't you? Did you think that God would hand you pieces of gold in a purse? Or an oil well?"

"Well, I did think he could work a miracle for me maybe. Is that wrong?"

"No. And I think he did work a miracle for you," Mama said firmly as she went to hang the dish towels on the line.

Matt went back to the porch steps and the *Dictionary of Thoughts.* He turned to Prayer again, looking for an answer to his question: Had God answered his prayer or had Windy John?

He found a quotation that interested him. "Prayer is merely a wish turned Godward." That made sense. He had gone to God with his greatest desire and God answered it through Windy John.

Matt looked at the quotation again and saw that it had been written by Phillips Brooks. Who was Phillips Brooks?

In another month he could walk into the Tansy High School library and find out.

John Paul and Vonnie came out to play "anti over the summer kitchen." John Paul caught the ball and ran around the building to tag his sister. She complained that the ball was lopsided and didn't bounce right.

John Paul laughed at her. "Put a little sugar on it," he crowed. She made a face at him, and they went back to their places.

Matt watched them tolerantly. With a high school in his future, who needed sugar? For that matter, who needed an oil well?